VANDALISM

The Not-So-Senseless Crime

by Arnold Madison

THE SEABURY PRESS · New York

FOR MY MOTHER
WHO ALWAYS KEEPS THE PORCH LIGHT ON
AND THE COFFEE POT PLUGGED IN
NO MATTER WHERE MY LATEST SCHEME TAKES ME

ACKNOWLEDGEMENTS

See page 143, which constitutes an extension of this copyright page.

Second Printing

Copyright © 1970 by Arnold Madison
Library of Congress Catalog Card Number: 70–125833

Design by Paula Wiener
Printed in the United States of America

Without Whom...

Traditional in nonfiction books is a list of acknowledgments the author wishes to include in the text. The custom is based on an undeniable fact: a book is never the product of only one person. *Vandalism* is no exception.

Surprisingly, not everyone wants his name placed in a book. Some people relate an anecdote and then quickly ask, "You won't mention my name, will you?" The reasons for the anonymity are often personal and obscure. There have been teen-agers and school employees and law enforcement officers who have all asked me that worried question.

No, I won't mention your names, but I do thank you.

An odd feeling comes over me every time I walk into a police station: a feeling of guilt for a crime I haven't committed. But two police departments quickly cleared me of that sensation. The Public Relations Department of the Nassau County Police Department was particularly helpful, providing me with press releases and tape recordings as well as opening their files to me. The men of the Juvenile Aid Bureau of the Suffolk County Police Department impressed me with their understanding of youngsters and their appreciation of juvenile problems. The children of Suffolk County are fortunate to have such men working in their behalf.

Chief George R. Collins of Auxiliary Police Unit 315 deposited into my hands a two-inch pile of papers and booklets during the several hours we talked in his office. He invited me to a meeting of the chiefs of all the auxiliary police units in Nassau County, thus opening up sources of information I would have missed. Finally, he permitted me to accompany himself and a patrolman on a "run" one frosty Saturday night.

But the pleasantest times of my research were the 87 degree afternoon and the snowy day after Christmas and the Friday night in a finished basement when I talked with teen-agers about vandalism. Now

Without Whom . . .

I know why some writers say they would much rather do research than do the writing. These youngsters treated *me* with such respect by giving me their confidences that I didn't want our talks to end. They entertained me with their sharp humor and impressed me with their sincerity. I am purposely listing their names alphabetically because all were equally important in providing a needed portion of the picture:

David Alvarez
Janet Diamond
Jane Doller
Dennis Gamble
Matt J. Gaudioso
Jane Goldschlager
Gary Haag
Zena Horowitz

Amy Leavitt
Linda Piacentini
Russell Rauf
Laurie Rothenberg
Michele Rothenberg
Tony Russo
Joanne Samuels
Melissa Young

And I want to express my gratitude to my editor, James Giblin, who from the first mention of the idea until the book's completion has given me the benefit of his clear thinking.

A. M.

Contents

Without Whom . . .   v

YESTERDAY

1. vandals and Vandals   3
2. Back Then and Over There   10

LAST NIGHT

3. Erosive Vandalism   25
4. Fun Vandalism   37
5. Angry Vandalism   48

Contents

TODAY

6. Community Reaction   69
7. Vigilantism and Auxiliary Police   85
8. Peer Reaction   99
9. The Laws and the Courts   110

TOMORROW

10. Some Answers   127

Sources and Suggested Readings   137
Index   145

x

"The teen-age vandal is a primary school child who breaks windows or a high school student who blows up mailboxes with a firecracker. He is a straight-A pupil or a consistent scholastic failure, police point out. He is the heir-apparent to a million dollars or the youngest of 13 poor children. He is sometimes a she."

—*Herald Statesman*
Yonkers, New York

1

vandals and Vandals

"It's time we stop.
Hey! What's that sound?
Everybody look what's going down."
                                    —*Stephen Stills*

In A.D. 406, an East German tribe, the Vandals, surged across the Rhine River into Gaul and set forth on a migration which would carry them over the Pyrenees to Spain and ultimately on to Carthage on the northern shore of Africa. From there the fleet of the Vandals preyed on the ships in the Mediterranean Sea while on land they persecuted the African Orthodox Christians. Their armies made plundering expeditions to Sicily and southern Italy, ravaging, burning, destroying.

The Vandals were not a creative people. They left no statues or monuments to their civilization, but

3

they did bequeath to us their name which conveys the hatred felt toward them by the Romans and the African Catholics. The ancient Vandals were adult warriors who accepted brutality as a way of life. Today's vandals for the most part have not yet reached the age where they may legally vote.

In October 1969, six boys, ranging in ages from 6 to 10, broke into a Cambridge, Massachusetts, scientific institute. They sprayed the laboratory with a fire extinguisher, poured chemicals over the valuable files, and released more than 2,000 specially-bred hamsters. The animals were products of years of planned breeding so that they could aid research on possible cancer-producing chemicals and help determine the role of chemical cyclamates, used in artificial sweeteners, in causing heart trouble.

Hundreds of hamsters scurried through the streets, and bodies of others were found floating in the Charles River. Many animals, stomped and mutilated to death, were scattered throughout the building. Dr. Freddy Homburger, the director of Bio-Research Institute, estimated that it would take two or three years to replace the destroyed hamsters at a cost of $100,000 a year.

The question is: why would children raised in a country with the highest standard of living in the world act like ancient barbarians? Why the senseless killing and destruction? Part of the answer is that even though we have supposedly become more civilized in the past fifteen hundred years, the name of the game is the same. Vandalism. And we are all losing—to the amount of "hundreds of millions of dollars yearly. And the cost is mounting steadily," according to the *U.S. News & World Report.* Amazingly, the general population appears indifferent.

At first glance the indifference seems understandable. A defaced stop sign is insignificant when compared to a population explosion, the future food shortage, and imminent nuclear destruction literally hanging over our heads. Yet it is almost impossible to pick up a newspaper without reading about incidents of destruction:

SCHOOL DAMAGED BY BOMB
                    —*Los Angeles Times*

MOTORCYCLE GANG WRECKS LI BAR
                    —*Newsday*

VANDALS ATTACK CHURCH IN SUBURB
                    —*New York Times*

Vandals and vandalism. As emotionally laden as the terms are, the attitude toward the rapidly growing problem is one of complacency. Possibly it is as Paul Goodman writes in *Like a Conquered Province,* "People believe that the great background con-

5

ditions of modern life are beyond our power to influence." This feeling of being overwhelmed by society's problems may explain the passivity of one South Shore community on Long Island.

Here is a postwar school district of six elementary schools, two junior high schools, a high school, and one of the highest tax rates on Long Island. When budget voting time neared, a decision was reached to eliminate several junior high school teaching positions. This way less money would be allocated to staff salaries. In order to do this, the school superintendent changed the educational policy of having two daily English classes for the junior high students who were deficient in reading and composition. Rather than the second period of English, sorely needed, the students would spend a free study-hall, forty minutes in the library. The announcement was made and received with no complaints. The community felt reassured that the school authorities were aware of the tremendous tax problem. The seven Board of Education members were more secure about their re-election. School leaders hoped that the budget would pass and an austerity budget would not be imposed upon them.

No outcry was heard that this district had paid $11,600 the previous year for window breakage. That sum would equal the salary of a teacher with a Master's Degree and at least ten years experience.

A teacher who would have helped many of these academically-poor students.

And the sum of $11,600 was only for windows. The school district had no way of computing the man hours put in by custodians to fix ripped-out sinks and chairs hurled down stairwells or repainting walls covered with spray paint obscenities.

Schools are not the only targets of vandals. Railroads, telephone companies, municipalities, state and national parks, all have startling wreckage costs. Individual families have not escaped, though no tally has been made of the private house windows which have to be replaced because late one night someone triggered an air pellet gun or hurled a stone. The average wage earner invariably pays all these bills.

Vandalism is widespread, cutting through all economic and social strata, and difficult to define. What is vandalism to one person might be spirited fun to another.

A street sign reading 30 M.P.H. has been changed so at first glance it appears to read 80 M.P.H. A joke? Roughly calculate the number of ruined signs in a county, and it becomes understandable why many Departments of Public Works have men whose sole job is to repaint defaced signs.

Fifteen hundred tombstones are toppled in Linden, New Jersey. A bunch of lively boys "horsing" around?

The bill was $35,000.

What about the dumping of commercial waste materials into our atmosphere and water? Consider the smog alerts in the Los Angeles area. Physical education classes in the schools are immediately canceled, and classroom teachers are told to give the children desk work. No exertion. Nothing which would cause the child to take deep lungfuls of the dangerous air. Lake Erie became another Dead Sea when the fish life was poisoned by the water pollution. Now the only surviving forms of life are sludge worms and a mutant species of carp that has adapted to the poison. Dr. Donald Squires, the director of the Marine Sciences Research Center at the State University of New York at Stony Brook, discovered the New York metropolitan area is annually depositing more sewage, garbage, and construction debris into the Atlantic than all the rivers on the East Coast wash into the ocean in a year. Can not businesses and cities be guilty of vandalism, too?

The scope of the problem *is* immense and therefore frightening, creating a feeling of hopelessness before an answer is sought. How can a situation of this magnitude be improved?

Not by ignoring it.

"Wherever violence is disregarded and forgotten, it perpetuates itself," wrote Dr. Fredric Wertham in *A Sign for Cain.*

Vandalism can be attacked by the same methods other social problems are approached. Define the problems. Look back for causative factors. Scan the present circumstances. Evaluate what solutions seem to be failing and which are succeeding. Arrive at a new possible plan of attack and begin working with that until proved right or wrong.

First, the definition.

Webster's Twentieth Century Dictionary defines vandalism as "willful destruction of the beautiful." As shown by the examples in this chapter, the contemporary problem is more extensive and pervasive, so it is necessary to broaden the meaning of the word.

In this book vandalism will mean *any willful act that lowers the esthetic or economic value of an object or area.*

Now to look back . . .

9

2

Back Then and Over There

"Those were the days, my friends"
—Gene Raskin

"Youth is disintegrating. The youngsters of the land have a disrespect for their elders and a contempt for authority in every form. Vandalism is rife, and crime of all kinds is rampant among our young people. The nation is in peril."

The quote is from *Young People and Crime* by Dr. Arthur H. Cain, and it is purportedly what an Egyptian priest said approximately four thousand years ago. What is interesting is not that people have always believed the young were rebellious—the irony has long left that fact—but that the crime is not a contemporary phenomenon. The forms of vandalism have probably changed, though. One has difficulty picturing an Athenian teen-ager of the Golden Age setting fire to the *Lyceum* or a twelfth century 16-year-old squire scrawling, "Make Love Not War" on the castle wall.

In *The History of Violence in America* Richard Maxwell Brown separates violence into Positive and Negative Violence. Negative Violence would be associated with feuds, lynching, prejudice, and urban riots. Positive Violence is a term that "relates violence to the popular and constructive movements" such as the Revolution, Civil War, Agrarian uprisings, Labor, etc. According to Brown's division, one of the earliest examples of vandalism in America would have to be labeled Positive Violence. The destruction not only made headlines. It made history.

The incident began when three ships sailed into Boston Harbor and docked at Long Wharf. The date was 1773. The ships' cargo: tea.

Boston was a tinderbox of conflicting loyalties. Some people considered the tea shipment a new attempt by the English prime minister, Lord North, to drain additional wealth from the colonies. Angry men gathered that cold night.

The Chronicles of the American Revolution, a compilation of remembrances of the Revolution, was collected in the early 1800's at the suggestion of John Adams. In the book is an account written by a man who was in Boston that December.

Vandalism

"The meeting [to protest the shipment] began at Faneuil Hall, but that place not being large enough it was adjourned to the Old South, and even that place would not contain all who came." A committee was selected and sent to the governor to ask him to have the ships set sail. Time passed slowly while those at the meeting hall waited. About sunrise the committee returned. The governor would not interfere.

Just then an Indian yell came from the street.

For a few startled moments the hall was silent, only to have everyone begin talking at once. People started to leave the hall. Samuel Adams claimed it was a trick by their enemies to disrupt the meeting and urged everyone to stay where they were. But the men rushed from the building to find an odd sight in the street. Many men had their faces smeared with lampblack or soot scraped from pots. A feather was stuck in each man's hair and blankets were wrapped about them Indian-style. Members of the Old South meeting accompanied the sixty to eighty "Indians" to the ships.

". . . nothing was destroyed but tea—and this was not done with noise and tumult . . . little or nothing being said by the agents or the multitude— who looked on. The impression was that of solemnity rather than of riot and confusion."

Three hundred and forty-five chests of tea were

dumped into the murky waters of Boston Harbor.

Not many years later Boston Harbor was again the scene of a vandal's attack. Once more the incident made headlines and caused considerable debate. The year was 1834, and the attack centered around one ship, *Old Ironsides*. The worn-out figurehead of Hercules had to be replaced. When the new one was set into place, people noticed that the face strongly resembled Andrew Jackson, then president of the United States. Naturally, the Democrats applauded the figurehead while anti-Jacksonites felt that *Old Ironsides* had been desecrated.

On the stormy night of July 2, a lone person sculled through the choppy water and pelting rain. About midnight he clambered up the side and decapitated the controversial head below the nose and ears. When the news broke, the entire country took sides. Ironically, when the culprit was found, he turned out to be a Jackson *supporter*. The reason for his attack? He was afraid anti-Democrats would damage *Old Ironsides* if the figurehead remained on the prow.

Notably, both crimes were politically motivated and accomplished by grown men. Some volunteers in the Boston Tea Party were rumored to be in their late teens, but that age was considered manhood at the time. In the early history of our country there were seemingly no incidents of what people today inaccurately call "senseless vandalism": destruction of property for no apparent reason. Any damage that occurred was associated with civil or political causes.

As the years passed and the country grew and became urbanized, vandalism still did not rank as a major problem.

1858: Minnesota became a state. Abraham Lincoln and Stephen Douglas engaged in a series of debates during their Senatorial Campaigns. That year seven people were convicted of Malicious Mischief (vandalism) in New York City. 2 females, 5 males. In 1965 there were 2,330 cases of Malicious Mischief in the city.

1865: The Civil War was won and a great leader lost. Lewis Carroll's *Alice's Adventures in Wonderland* was published. A *New York Times* editorial proclaimed: "DECREASE OF JUVENILE CRIME —An Encouraging Sign." The three principal offenses of minors were listed: vagrancy, petit larceny, and pocket-picking.

1872: In that year Thomas Edison perfected the "duplex" telegraph, and the *New York Times* editorialized, "It is evident that offenses against property most prevail in youths and that the ruling motives to it are the love of enjoyment and idleness with the dislike of labor and the pressure of want."

So as the nineteenth century faded and the twentieth century dangled a promise of progress and unsuspected wonders before the world, vandalism was barely noticed. In rural communities the problem did not exist. One of the theories explaining the epidemic of vandalism today is that young people are affected by the anonymity and depersonalization of city and suburban living. In a village at the turn of the century, the children did not feel this. Everyone knew what everyone was doing. A person was a part of the whole, and he or she recognized this from the earliest years.

Thornton Wilder captured the atmosphere of small town America in his play, *Our Town*. On a moonlit night that brings everyone to their windows to dream and think, two men meet on a corner. One is Constable Warren, walking his nightly tour.

> MR. WEBB: Oh, Bill—if you see my boy smoking just give him a word will you? He thinks a lot of you, Bill.
> CONSTABLE WARREN: I don't think he smokes no cigarettes, Mr. Webb. Leastways not more'n two or three a year.

Such was life in Grover's Corners, New Hampshire, May 7, 1901.

The first year that vandalism appears as a heading in a *New York Times Index* volume is 1920, and then only a cross reference. The graves of writer Johann Goethe and dramatist Johann Schiller had been robbed in Germany. The following year a sole item was listed under the heading of Vandalism. The date: October 15, 1921.

The school board in Spring Valley, New York, offered a $25 reward for the vandal who had cut a hole in the high school cornerstone and had stolen the copper box set inside the granite block. The person broke through the cornerstone, which had been laid in 1916, by cutting a hole the size of the box from the basement side. The opening had been cemented up after the metal container was stolen. In the box were $10 worth of coins, historic school records, and copies of local newspapers. So the first legitimate listing for vandalism in the *New York Times Index* was truly prophetic, as schools have since become the prime target of vandals.

1936 was a good year for some women and a bad one for others. Margaret Mitchell had her best seller *Gone With the Wind* published, and an aviatrix, Mrs. A. Mollison, flew from England to Capetown, South Africa, in 3 days, 6 hours, 26 minutes. But in Union, New Jersey, the local police finally apprehended the individual who for a month had daubed paint on street signs and school walls. Police cars, also, had been smeared with painted phrases such as "Boy Scout Taxi" and "Puppet Cars." The culprit, apprehended fittingly enough in the police station parking lot, was a 20-year-old blonde. She was caught literally red-handed: clutching a can of red paint and two brushes. When questioned about the reason for her vandalistic acts, she told the police she was gathering material for a book!

Books and women figured in the disclosure of another minor act of vandalism that year. Lady Ravensdale, daughter of Marquess Curzon, was following the route that her travelogue-writer father had traveled through Asia Minor in the eighteen-eighties. There on the gateway to the palace of Darius, she found scratched into the stone, "G. N. Curzon 1889." She was shocked to find her father "had committed such an outrage."

If 1936 was disillusioning to Lady Ravensdale, the next decade saw juvenile crime and, in particular, vandalism take a large leap toward today's level. During World War II family life was not only disrupted, it was shattered. The fathers were off fighting the war while many mothers were riveting dural on P-48 Thunderbolts. As a result numerous children roamed the streets at night. One community, Hastings-on-Hudson, New York, had a serious problem of broken windows, punctured automobile tires, as well as stolen hubcaps and residence signs. The village passed an emergency ordinance which made it unlawful for the parents or guardians of children under 16 to permit the minors to be on the streets after 10:30 P.M. unless accompanied by an adult.

The ordinance was again invoked in February 1961 in an effort to stop widespread vandalism. If the police find a youngster under 16 out past the curfew, the parents are notified. The child is paroled the next morning in the parents' custody.

The same month in 1961 that an American town on the Hudson River was combatting vandalism, a Scottish community on Holy Loch had a similar problem due to Americans. The U.S. Polaris submarine tender, *Proteus*, was to arrive in Holy Loch. A group of English youths had gathered to protest the use of Great Britain's harbors for alien nuclear war machinery. The demonstrators planned to row out in five dinghies and two canoes and block the channel which the *Proteus* had to use in its approach. The night before the ship's arrival, sixteen young Scots raided the English camp and set the dinghies and canoes adrift.

In the early sixties many other vandalism reports coming from overseas were connected with political beliefs:

In Salisbury, England, BAN THE BOMB was painted on eight of the famous Stonehenge slabs in four-foot yellow letters. The ninth stone was marked with the emblem of the British campaign for Nuclear Disarmament, even though a branch of the organization claimed they had nothing to do with the vandalism.

Jakarta, Indonesia: Indonesian high school and university students attacked Chinese Communist diplomatic establishments, smashing furniture and files. Another group ransacked Peking's official press service office and set fire to the roof.

PRETORIA VANDALS ASSAIL U.S. headlined an article in the *New York Times*. Red hammers and sickles were painted on two U.S. diplomatic cars only a week after the U.S. insignia on the embassy building in South Africa had been sprayed with black paint as well as the phrase, "Yanks Out—We Don't Want Red Agitators."

The sentiment seems to echo one sprayed on a synagogue in Cologne, Germany, on Christmas Eve, 1959. "Germans demand that Jews Get Out." The entire problem of anti-Semitic vandalism is like an echo in Germany, a lingering cry of hate.

Hersbruck: Nazi emblems were chiseled into a memorial honoring concentration camp victims.

Bamberg: The city had planned to dedicate a memorial on the site of a synagogue burned by the Nazis. The night before the ceremony the granite slab was smeared with a yellow swastika and the slogan, *Judas Verrecke* (Die, Judas). Officials summoned workmen to clean up the mess and kept the incident quiet. Two nights later, however, the vandals splashed swastikas on 23 gravestones in the Jewish cemetery. Non-Jewish youth groups laid wreaths inscribed "Forgive us, Brothers" at the desecrated headstones, and the city marshaled police and civilian guards to stand watch over the property of the city's seventy Jewish inhabitants. The anti-Semites, however, struck twice more.

Berlin: In November 1968, the new Berlin National Gallery opened. The Gallery had been designed by a refugee from Nazi Germany. One night nine swastikas were painted on the walls and on works of sculpture outside the Gallery by three men using spray cans of paint.

In the late 1960's nonpolitical vandalism became prevalent in Europe and the Middle East, ending the belief that America has the worst juvenile crime in the world. In fact, according to Dr. Arthur H. Cain in *Young People and Crime*, our juvenile delinquency rate is not the highest. We are surpassed by Japan and Sweden. Israel, too, has a soaring rate of youthful lawbreakers.

In October 1965, there were two riots during one week in Tel Aviv, involving approximately 1,000 teen-agers. Dr. Judith T. Shuval of The Israel Institute of Applied Social Research has set forth some reasons for Israel's youth crime problem, and the explanations sound like ones touted in this country. First, an increasingly affluent society. Dr. Shuval claims that the young people are rebelling against authority and "stealing automobiles is a classic example of this." Also, immigrant children coming into the country see the affluence gap, resent it, and are spurred into criminal activities. Family structure is changing, too, from large, cohesive paternal groups to the Western-type small family units. And lastly, Dr. Shuval points out that the overall values of the country are being altered as the challenges facing earlier immigrants disappear.

Reports of other recent foreign teen-age vandalism sound identical to American incidents.

August 31, 1968. Teen-agers went on a rampage in several coastal resorts, causing heavy damage. Hundreds of boys and girls spent the night on the beach, battled with police on the promenade, and threw bottles at cars or through shop windows.

This is not the annual invasion of college students into Fort Lauderdale, Florida, but rather Margate, England, on the Channel Coast.

Another news item told of hundreds of leather-jacketed youths who went on a rampage and were arrested for drunkenness and theft.

Californian Hell's Angels? No. The youth of Bathurst, Australia.

Vandalism

An eastern city spent $18,000 in 1969 to clean graffiti off walls. Grenoble. In eastern France.

And so it goes.

Fans returning home Saturday nights from English soccer matches smash train windows or rip up the seats, reminiscent of Madison Square Garden fight fans and New York City subways. Two thousand youths riot in Oslo, Norway, when the police decide to close a favorite club. A girl in Oxford, England, died because her father could not use a vandalized pay phone to call a doctor. More than half of Britain's 75,000 pay phones are struck by vandals. The statue of the Little Mermaid in Copenhagen's harbor was decapitated one night by vandals. Fortunately, the 50-year-old mold had been preserved, allowing Edvard Erickson's original metal statue to be restored.

At different rates of speed, vandalism has traveled the same route the world over. Destruction began as political or social protests for easily discerned reasons. As the affluence of modern life has spread, however, the motivation has become harder to identify.

The following three chapters explore some of the causes of modern day vandalism.

LAST NIGHT

3

Erosive Vandalism

"Please don't destroy these lands
Don't make them desert sands."
                    —*Samwell-Smith–Relf–McCarthy*

Imagine a six-foot high statue, the lines gracefully
depicting the beauty of the human body, the marble
glistening. One morning the figure is set in a lush
corner of the city park. Seven-year-old Kevin ambles
by on his way to school and spots the newly erected
statue. The sparkling white marble is unblemished.
And Kevin knows that many people will be passing
this statue. Using his crayons, he scrawls his initials,
a large red K. S., on the right foot.

Shortly after, a young married couple stop and
after a moment's study, decide that the whole left
arm would make a marvelous conversation piece for

their new circular coffee table. And the city certainly has enough money to fix this statue with all the taxes they pay! One whack with a thick log and the white arm is theirs.

In the afternoon two boys returning from a baseball game see the mutilated statue and conclude a little more damage will not be noticed. For a half-hour, they practice pitching by hurling rocks at specially selected targets on the marble body.

Late that evening as three college boys are wending their way home from a fraternity party, bottles in hand, they spot the statue. The wine bottle is half empty, the two beer bottles completely drained, so they will have to get rid of them anyway. Each guy can have one throw. The brown bottles go astray, crunching into the underbrush, but the wine bottle smashes against the stone chin, dribbling wine down the length of the statue. The boys continue on, arms slung around each other's shoulders, singing their college alma mater.

As the first rays of sunlight strike the statue the following morning, a park department man notices the pock-marked, red-streaked figure and makes a note to tell his superior to do something about having the unsightly statue removed.

The above fictional account may seem an exaggeration, but when magnified many times, it is actually what is happening in our country. Erosive

Vandalism. Tiny acts of destruction that in themselves are not very damaging or costly or shocking, but when combined are in effect wearing away this nation's natural and man-made resources. Consider the tons of paper and trash thrown into our city streets and country roads or the thousands of road signs either defaced or mutilated with bullet holes or the smashed park benches and the store-front windows peppered with tiny holes from BB pellets. Each of these bits of destruction by itself is easy to ignore because the damage seems small and unimportant, but, cumulatively, the drain on our economy is enormous.

Ironically, much ruination is done by people who do not feel that they are guilty of a crime. The individuals may be aware of the laws prohibiting certain actions, but they feel that the rules are unrealistic. What could be wrong, they ask, about picking up a rock chip in the Petrified Forest National Park? There are acres and acres of the petrified wood. The people do not stop to imagine what would happen if each of the millions of annual visitors to the site walked off with only one stone.

"We didn't do nothin' wrong," teen-agers say defensively. "Only messed around a little. No big thing."

We didn't do nothin' wrong?

The Western Electric Telephone Company invests

more than four million dollars a year, keeping phones repaired that have been knocked out by theft or vandalism. There are 3,600 sidewalk phones in New York City, most of which suffer from looted coin boxes, tipped-over booths, smashed glass or plastic panes, and stolen parts. One vandal strolled down Park Avenue, methodically severing the receiver on outdoor phones by melting the connecting wire with a cigarette lighter. He placed the receiver on the booth shelf and went on to the next phone. Nothing was stolen, only ruined. Edward A. Connell, the general manager of the public telephone department, told the *New York Times*, "It's a constant battle. And one where the offense is always catching up with the defense."

No big thing?

Two men died in Pawtucket, Rhode Island, as a result of vandalism. One night teen-agers pulled down a metal fence and dragged it into a drainage pool. A crane was needed to hoist the fence from the water. Two workers in their early twenties seized the fence at the same moment the crane came in contact with a 13,800-volt wire overhead. The electricity flowed through the crane and fence, electrocuting the men.

Undoubtedly, if the vandals had known what was going to happen, they would not have wrecked the fence. That is the difficulty. No one can be certain where vandalism will lead. In October 1969, Bronx youths in two cars hurled stones at a house wall and windows several times during the evening and early morning hours. The 19-year-old resident rushed from the building with a rifle. Fortunately, before any serious crime could be committed, he was stopped.

But how can we stop Erosive Vandalism? In order to answer that, it is necessary to understand the causes. Many explanations are offered as to why people seem to have a no-care attitude about public property. On an abstract level, the depersonalization of our environment is held to blame. Critics maintain that small-town America was never afflicted with the degree of vandalism which abounds in the country today. The quiet, tree-lined streets and small business districts with the familiar, friendly shop owners formed roots for the young people. The teen-agers felt a part of the town and did not want to destroy it.

"Now, in Northern Ohio, anyway, it is all gone— buried under supermarkets, superhighways, urban development, . . . real estate coups, civic reforms, discount houses, hamburger franchises. The land and the people are now permanently separated." So observed Arnold Kazmier in a September 1969 article in *The Village Voice*.

If the land and the people are truly separated,

29

then it is no wonder that young people and adults alike feel no reticence about disfiguring or destroying the land. It is not their land. Its beauty means nothing to them other than a passing view.

An experiment conducted by two psychologists, Scott Fraser and Philip Zimbardo, added further evidence to the theory that the anonymity of an environment has a direct effect on vandalism.

At 3:15 one Friday afternoon they left a 1959 green Oldsmobile parked along a street in a middle-class, residential neighborhood of New York City. The license plates were removed and the hood slightly opened so it would look as if the car had been stolen or left alone while its owner went for help. The two men hid themselves where they could observe and note what happened to the car. Ten minutes later a man and a wife and a son came driving by, parked, and took a hacksaw from their own car. They cut out the Oldsmobile's battery and also took the radiator.

By the end of twenty-six hours the following had been removed from the car in addition to the battery and the radiator: air cleaner, radio antenna, windshield wipers, the right-hand side chrome strip, hubcaps, a set of jumper cables, a gas can, a container of car wax, the left rear tire (others too worn).

The car stripping took place in daylight and was done by clean-cut, well-dressed, middle-class people. The theft of major items and the destruction was almost always observed by someone else who sometimes carried on a casual conversation with the vandals.

Another car was parked in a similar condition, but this time the automobile was left on a street in a quiet, settled Californian suburb. Three days later nothing had been touched. Why would people living in a city be more inclined to destruction and theft than suburban residents?

Fraser and Zimbardo labeled the cause "deindividuation": the process by which many former restraints in American life are being dissolved. In a big city the feeling of personal anonymity encourages violent behavior. City inhabitants have learned "not to get involved," so they step around the drunk sleeping on the sidewalk. Lawbreakers feel certain that people will not interfere unless directly involved. On the other hand, vandalism is discouraged by a sense of community, an atmosphere in which vandals feel someone is watching and will disapprove. There is much more danger that people will stop a criminal or call authorities in this type of setting.

Capitalizing on the theory that there will be less vandalism if wrongdoers have the feeling they are under surveillance, the police department in Nassau County, New York, has instituted a Neighborhood

Security Program. Householders are urged to join the NSP by simply agreeing to help each other protect their person and property. If a resident should see a crime being committed or any suspicious action, he would call the police.

"We don't ask or want members of the Neighborhood Security Program to take enforcement action," said Nassau Police Commissioner Francis B. Looney. "That's our job. The Neighborhood Security Program achieves its goal when neighbors become alert to the activities in their neighborhood and call the police immediately."

The NSP is similar to a plan operating in New Canaan, Connecticut, as described by David Loth in *Crime in the Suburbs*. This program was organized specifically to combat youth crime. The town has set up an underground auxiliary of citizens who report secretly any juvenile they see breaking the law. The police chief hoped that the knowledge that someone might be looking would make youngsters think twice before engaging in vandalism.

Both police plans are designed to combat the depersonalized atmosphere of contemporary living. Unfortunately, they are only stopgap programs because they are not changing the basic situation.

While the problem of "deindividuation" is difficult for the average person to overcome, there is another cause of Erosive Vandalism which might be corrected. The inadvertent teaching of disrespect of public property by parents. Here is an incident this writer observed. A father and his two children climbed into the family car, the daughter munching on an apple. As the car motor warmed up in the driveway, the girl finished the apple and rolled down the rear window to throw out the core.

"Not here," snapped her father. "Wait till we get out on the road."

Many parents think the way to teach children is to instruct or give them directives to live by, when actually children learn most through observing their mother and father. The girl now knows that it's perfectly all right to litter the streets. As she grows into her teens, will she be like the vandal who visited a park in the western part of the United States? Park officials found a lipstick heart and initials drawn on an ancient Indian rock carving. The lipstick penetrated the minute pores in the stone and could not be removed. The etchings had survived hundreds of years of weather and erosion and history, only to be marred by a family's vacation trip. Why shouldn't our apple-eater commit such an offense in future years? The park is not her property. It's out on the road.

The problem of graffiti has other causes. Psychologists say it is a need to be recognized, to stand out from the crowd, to be noticed. Or in some cases, to be immortalized even on a small scale. Man is the only animal who consciously knows he is going to die, so he does things which will be here after he is dead. Climb the 500-foot Great Pyramid and absorb the golden Egyptian sunset. Scratched into the rocks high above the desert sands are centuries-old names and dates of other visitors. They remain, though the people are gone.

The presence of graffiti was solved in Oakland, California, though not by the city officials. A 60-foot tunnel that leads into the 44-acre Lake Temescal Park for the convenience of vehicles and pedestrians had long been a target for vandals. The walls were covered with 30-odd years of obscene and unsightly scrawls. Park maintenance men would paint out the graffiti, only to have it reappear a short time later.

A Dominican monk became aware of the situation and decided to correct it. He splashed bright red and yellow designs over the walls. Sprightly free-form green trees and abstract orange blossoms as well as birds, fish, and sails decorated the tunnel. Since then hardly a mark has been placed on the walls except the names of a boy and girl which were printed neatly beneath two bluebirds romantically sharing a branch.

The ugliness is gone because someone cared.

But much ugliness still exists in this country and not enough people seem to care. Litter. And it comes in all forms. Walk by the river which curves along the Yosemite Valley floor. Beer cans and broken soda bottles and a rusting bicycle frame clutter the sandy river bottom. Our city streets have toppling piles of garbage in front of restaurants, poorly packaged, spilling forth their contents of rotting foodstuffs. And it isn't only individuals. We pick up a newspaper and learn that only sixteen miles from downtown Denver a plant manufacturing triggers for atomic devices may have been poisoning the ground and the air with radioactive plutonium, one of the most toxic materials produced by man.

Litter, on all levels of meaning, is a social problem created by society. We want ease and comfort, so manufacturers put products in disposable containers. As a result we "dispose" of them along our highways and into our trash pails. Sanitation departments inherit the problem. New plastic containers do not rot, and the new glass does not burn, so town dumps and incinerators are collecting growing piles of rubbish while available land is shrinking. Dumping the waste into oceans seemed an answer, but now the sea near large cities has growing areas of pollution that threaten sea life and recreational facilities.

Affluence permits us to buy more things more quickly. At one time families kept automobiles until the vehicles developed serious problems that required expensive repairs. Now cars are traded in after only a few years, their owners wanting sleeker, shinier models. Recently, *Vermont Life* magazine detailed that state's plans to eliminate the problem of abandoned automobiles. The New England state identified with rolling green mountains and farms and white steepled churches was in danger of becoming an automobile graveyard.

Our country, too, is in danger. And the danger is Erosive Vandalism—the crime that will reduce the nation to an ugly, scarred wasteland unless people on all levels begin to care.

4

Fun Vandalism

"Everybody knows there's nothing doing
Everything is closed, it's like a ruin."
—*Lennon–McCartney*

People often shrug off reports about the rise in vandalism, saying, "Boys will be boys." Fathers chuckle knowingly and relate an adventurous episode from their own teen years. In *Kids, Crime and Chaos*, Roul Tunley wrote that misbehaving youngsters were the ones who were interested in adventure, change, risk, and excitement.

The search for adventure is echoed in the result of the research done by Sheldon and Eleanor Glueck. This husband and wife team of psychologists devised a test for very young children in order to predict the potential delinquents. They found that delinquents had an "excessive thirst for adventure." The key word is excessive. Certainly no one wants a child who is timid or so bound by society that he is content to live his life in the same path cut by his parents.

Yet it appears that adventure, fun, getting-something-going can lead to destruction. "They will do anything in order to do something," the Cleveland, Ohio, *Plain Dealer* quoted Juvenile Court Judge Albert A. Waldman. One vandal gave as a reason for his misbehavior when interviewed by the *New York Times*, "Did it for kicks."

The destruction just happens. A side effect to a good time. No harm intended really. It's all a kind of joke. A laugh.

Fun Vandalism.

A small mining town nestled in the North Dakota hills has the unlikely name, Zap, and an approximate population of three hundred. This back hills hamlet acquired instant fame one weekend in May 1969.

Weeks before the fateful night, the North Dakota State University student newspaper urged readers to "zip to Zap" for a Mother's Day "Zap-Out." The idea sparked a flame which swept from Florida to Toronto. Cars bearing signs reading "Zap or Bust" prepared for the journey to the town that lay seventy miles northwest of Bismarck. The mayor of Zap, Norman Fuchs, was photographed wearing a sweatshirt inscribed, "Zap, N.D. or Bust."

"I'm certain it will be the biggest day in our history," he announced prophetically.

The Zappians readied themselves for the gala event. Along the unpaved main street, the café and two bars stocked up for the expected customers. Lucky's Bar stacked thousands of extra cans of beer in the back room. No one seemed particularly disturbed by rumors that the college students were going to make Zap "The Fort Lauderdale of the North." That Florida city is plagued with mobs of troublemaking college students whenever vacation times come.

By late Friday night as 2,500 people crowded into town, the temperature dropped to the low forties. When a few beers had rinsed away the wearying effects of the trip, the students ignited a bonfire in the main street. An abandoned frame house was dismantled, its doors, siding, and window frames providing fuel for the flames. Booths and tables were ripped from the taverns to keep the fire roaring.

As the temperature and spirits climbed higher and higher around the fire, store windows were smashed and the merchandise scattered. With odds of three against one, there was little the townspeople could do to halt the mob. In the Community Hall, the wallboard was shredded, and the soft drink machine pilfered. A fire truck was called to douse the fire but as the vehicle reached the spot, scores of youths climbed aboard and began to rip it apart. An automobile near the bonfire area was wrecked by 500 students.

Mayor Fuchs wandered through his town, muttering, "Animals, animals."

The governor sent in 500 National Guardsmen, combat-ready, with rifles and five-foot clubs. Within an hour of the troops' appearance, the students had fled. The small café had sales of $150 for that Friday night and damages totaling $2,000 by the next morning. Not one store could open for business Saturday.

No one would argue that the students' behavior was anything but reprehensible. No one would dismiss such destruction as youthful exuberance. Yet the motivation for minor league hi-jinks and for a Zap-type riot are the same.

Psychologically, when a person destroys a piece of property, he is in effect destroying the owners. Or as Paul Goodman wrote in *Growing Up Absurd*, "To do the forbidden is to attack the forbidding authority." So youngsters who are restrained by many elements of society find enjoyment in freeing themselves of these bonds by attacking society's possessions. Rare is the joy that matches the joy of gaining one's freedom, and the teen years are the time when children yearn for independence. "Vandalism is inherent in the nature of the adolescent," said

Solomon Lichter, the director of the Scholarship and Guidance Association.

Allied with this desire for liberty is the sense of power an individual experiences when doing something in a group. Young people badgered by school officials and parents find themselves in control once they are in a crowd. Today, most adults feel a tinge of apprehension when near a large group of teenagers. We are a country afraid of our children. And the youngsters know this. In a group *they* can give the orders. Youth Power. And the power knows no limits as long as the crowd is large enough.

Law enforcement officers appreciate the dangers of congregated young people.

A Juvenile Aid Bureau detective for the Suffolk County Police Department, New York, described vandalism as a "group activity."

"Warm months are the worst time for vandalism. When kids can get out in hoards," said a member of the Nassau County Police Department, when asked about the peak periods for vandalism.

Railroad employees agree. With the advent of spring weather attacks on trains across the country become more frenzied. The Grand Trunk Western Railroad suffered a $248,000 derailment because vandals wrecked switches near Grand Rapids, Michigan. The New Haven Railroad, which has to replace 4,000 windows a year, finds that gangs of hooligans

41

engaging in rock throwing, tampering with switches, and depositing objects on the rails sprout with the new buds. Sometimes trains are attacked Indian-style with the rock hurlers lining each side of the tracks. Commuters can only sit there helplessly, shielding their faces with newspapers or ducking down in their seats as the train runs the gamut. The crew radioes ahead and summons the company's private policemen, but these officers only have the power of arrest on railroad property and usually arrive too late.

April showers not only bring May flowers but May fires. Volunteer suburban fire departments brace themselves for the spate of fires in parks, as well as wooded sections along freeways and parkways, which occur once warm weather encourages youngsters to spend most of the daylight hours outside.

"These kids think it's a joke to set a fire and then wait nearby to see how long it takes us to get there. On weekends [in the spring] we sometimes get as many as twenty-five calls," revealed one fire fighter.

Though groups of young people can be a source of trouble, the amount of vandalism still exceeds the psychological potential. "Are we to say that young boys, brimming with energy, curious about life, eager for action, have no way to channel all these things except to roam about and destroy what strikes their fancy to destroy?" editorialized *The Evening Statesmen* of Boise, Idaho.

There *are* other ways to channel these drives, but, ironical as it may seem, the children have been educated to enjoy destruction, to look forward to the time when they can wander the streets, leaving a trail of wreckage behind them. An even more bitter truth is that they have been educated by their families.

Halloween.

"The night when the world goes crazy," said an auxiliary police patrolman.

And so it must seem to any law enforcement officer.

The night of October 31st has long been reserved for children and mischief. Years ago youngsters might steal Mrs. Leroy's pumpkin or rub soap on Mr. Henderson's car windows. But these activities were never condoned by the adult world.

Today parents, fearful their children will miss something, take pre-school youngsters dressed in costumes the children can not comprehend and lead them down suburban streets. The mother or father stands at the curb, arms folded, and urges the child to climb the steps and ring the bell. The youngster does this, still puzzled.

The good work done by children on Halloween for UNICEF should not be overlooked. Nickels and dimes are collected for needy children the world over. But if a child starts tricking or treating at the age of four, is it not to be expected that he will be bored with this activity by the time he is ten and think it too childish for someone his age? Some youngsters will want to advance to something more exciting. And the same parents who dragged their toddlers around apparently have no hesitation about letting their older children roam town after dark on Halloween. Parents usually tell the youths, "Now don't do anything wrong."

"What the hell do they think the kids are doing?" the auxiliary patrolman asked an interviewer.

A good question. Why do these parents think, for several weeks before Halloween, press releases and spot radio announcements are made by the local police? For example: one by the Nassau County Police.

Commissioner Looney also advised parents to warn their children—especially teen-agers—that Halloween festivities do not include the wanton destruction of property. Anyone maliciously damaging property will be liable to arrest for criminal mischief, and if the malicious mischief is against a mailbox the crime is a Federal offense.

County police will more than double patrols on Halloween day and evening, and patrolmen and detectives of the Youth Division will intensify their operations in unmarked patrol cars.

Halloween pranks today are far more serious than soap on the windows. Cars are streaked with irremovable spray paint, town flagpoles are bent in two, teen-age gangs block intersections, jumping on roofs or hoods of trapped cars and terrorizing the women drivers with shouted obscenities and lewd gestures.

If police apprehend a youngster, they can be fairly certain that once they locate the parents, the mother and father will enter the station house angry at the *police*.

The same child whose mother encourages him to enjoy Halloween to the fullest from the earliest may have a father who one week attends a business or fraternal convention. As American males travel to convention cities, they often seem to retrogress in time with each mile. They may board a train mature men, the sole supports for their wives and children, but by the time they reach their destination, they are wearing paper hats and tooting noisemakers. Their meeting days are filled with boyish pranks, or, as in the case of the state volunteer firemen's convention recently held in Buffalo, New York, harassment and vandalism provided the entertainment.

Staying in the Statler-Hilton Hotel on the 14th and 15th floors was a traveling group of Japanese, promoting Expo '70, the world's fair in Osaka, Japan. Four young women were with the Japanese party. The visiting firemen had rooms on most floors of the hotel. According to Richard Murphy, the public relations representative for the Japanese entourage, "The firemen pounded on the doors of the women's rooms on Sunday night and used language which was frightening and objectionable to the women." In addition, the Buffalo *Courier-Express* reported that the delegates had dropped soap powder into a memorial fountain which had been erected in honor of the assassinated President William McKinley, who was murdered in Buffalo in 1901.

When conventioneers go home, they repeat the exciting goings-on to their friends. Their children hear and are impressed. Just as children of smoking parents are more likely to start smoking before children of nonsmokers, youngsters will want to emulate misbehaving parents. Maybe some day they can grow up and have fun like Dad! Why wait till then? Let's have some fun right now! Should we then be surprised when soap is dumped into the geysers of Yellowstone National Park by teen-agers and the holes are stuffed with sticks and logs?

A child, also, hears stories from his older brother. "We had a couple drinks at a party," a boy told the *New York Times,* "then got hopped up on pot and went out in a car to have some fun." This focuses attention on another facet of the vandalism problem. The increased mobility of youth aids vandals. Park officials in the Western states are plagued with cars filled with teen-agers who have been drinking. The youngsters drive through the park areas, disturbing campers and wrecking property, and are gone before they can be apprehended. When a pre-teen-ager hears this type tale from an older brother or sister, he thinks that the sooner he starts acting like that, the sooner he will be like his big brother.

"Destruction is sometimes copied from the high school to the junior high school because brothers go home and tell little brothers. Some families are just rotten," confided a 15-year-old girl from Syosset, New York.

Parents should accept the fact that a child is a product of his environment. Controlling the outside influences on a son or daughter is difficult, but mothers, fathers, brothers, and sisters comprise the family unit which is the single most powerful factor affecting a growing child.

All of us might bear in mind that Fun Vandalism is caused by several factors: a few intrinsic to the adolescent, others induced by misguided outsiders. The search for fun can lead to spontaneous vandalism, but we have to be careful that we do not dismiss vandalism as boyish fun. If adults make light of the crime, then they certainly cannot expect children and young people to take prevention campaigns seriously.

5

Angry Vandalism

"You're stompin' my mind . . ."
—Heend–Ross

The third type of vandalism seems more understand-able, though still inexcusable: destruction motivated by anger.

To cite an example. Mr. and Mrs. John H. Ryan, whose two daughters are victims of cerebral palsy, do volunteer work for the United Cerebral Palsy Association of Nassau County, New York. Once a year the Ryans held a fund-raising "South Seas Night" in their backyard, inviting friends, co-work-ers, parents of afflicted children. Stores contributed the makings for the fish and clam dinner, and neigh-bors helped Mrs. Ryan prepare the meal.

On one such Friday night, they raised more than $1,000 for CP from a gathering of about 300 people who had paid ten dollars a couple. The four-piece band and the bright lights coupled with the possibility of free beer was a magnet, attracting some uninvited teen-agers.

"There were three or four or maybe four or five of them," Ryan later said. "I didn't see them. They were making remarks to some of the women, and a couple of our men told them to leave. I understand that they [the teen-agers] said, 'We're going to get shotguns and clean the place out.'"

The benefit ended shortly after 2 A.M. The next day, Saturday, neighbors helped with the clean-up activities. About eleven-thirty that evening, the Ryans and a few friends were sitting in the Ryan backyard, enjoying the balmy night and discussing how badly the CP Association needed the collected money.

"While I was coming out with a tray of food, five cars loaded with kids came by," Mrs. Ryan told a local newspaper. "It was like a funeral procession. There was one boy in the front car, hanging out of the window up to his waist and pointing with his finger as if he was saying, 'This is the place.' I knew [who they were]. I ran."

The men stayed outside while a neighbor rushed for help. Mrs. Ryan telephoned the police and hurried into the bedroom where her third child, a five-year-old daughter with a spinal ailment, was sleeping. A moment after the mother had snatched the girl from the bed, a picnic bench crashed through the window, spraying glass onto the sheets and blankets.

Outside, some of the twenty-five youths surrounded a neighbor and pounded him with trash cans. A second man was beaten with a rake so severely that he later needed six stitches to close a scalp wound. Other attackers smashed picnic tables, and still more boys hurled bricks and garbage pails through windows and against the aluminum siding of the house.

Nearby residents, who later said they had thought a plane had crashed, came out of their homes. "The noise was deafening," Ryan's wife agreed.

When distant police sirens screamed that help was approaching, the boys fled to their waiting cars. "We fixed them. We fixed them good," one youth shouted triumphantly as he struggled into the crowded automobile. Rubber screeched on tar, and the gang was gone.

Shock still strained Mrs. Ryan's voice when she told police, "It [the attack] took less than two minutes."

As ugly as the realization is concerning how these boys' minds must work, we are able to trace the twisting thought patterns. In their off-course think-ing, the destruction was simply revenge for an insult.

Vandalism is not a senseless crime when the motivation is clear. If angry residents of East Harlem spend two hours throwing garbage into the streets, we do not view it as an unreasonable act, but rather a protest against the lack of garbage-collection serv-ices. When eight people including three members of the clergy admit that they invaded Selective Ser-vice offices, dumping and tearing up 75,000 files, the impetus for the anti-war action is evident. At 12:20 A.M. September 11, 1969, a homemade bomb ex-ploded on the window ledge of the Pacific Palisades High School, California. Damage to the administra-tion building was $20,000. Here, too, the motivation is obvious. Someone was angry at the school. We may be distressed by these deeds or we may sym-pathize with them, but we're not puzzled as to why they happened.

There are, however, incidents where the "why" is not easily discerned. Yet humans are rational crea-tures. We do things for a reason.

In Union Township, New Jersey, the windows of 250 parked cars were smashed. Also the fenders and doors were crumbled by two stolen cars that were purposely crashed into one parked car after another.

At whom were these vandals angry?

Certainly not 250 different people. In all likelihood

none of the automobile owners was known by the boys.

When we dissect the more subtle motivations for angry vandalism we begin to understand why the problem is so widespread. Say the car wreckers numbered five. The boys may have been angry for five different reasons, letting their hostility blend into one act. The April 1966 *New York Times* typified the average vandal as a white teen-age boy from a middle-income family, living in a suburb. The reason that these youths turned to vandalism is that the destruction of property is the delinquent behavior most available to a "nice kid" from a "nice neighborhood." So if five boys angry for different reasons decide to "get even," there is ample opportunity and little danger of being caught.

But why would a "nice kid" want to "get even"?

Research is not necessary to realize that today a youngster has to be much older than his counterpart of years ago before he is treated as an adult. He is not needed on the farm to do a man's work at planting or harvesting time. Laws requiring attendance in school and the lack of job opportunities make him dependent on his parents until a later age. Mothers and fathers often boast that their son doesn't "have to work like I did when I was his age," feeling that they have done well for their children. Yet the boy suffers from this period of limbo.

A teen-age boy approaches manhood eagerly. He wants a manly job both for the income and a feeling of self-importance. The first goal is consciously expressed, the second sensed. Money gives independence, the chance to buy the clothes *he* prefers, the phonograph records *he* enjoys, to date without having to beg his father for money. The knowledge that he has tackled a difficult job and done it well affords him pleasure and helps strengthen his self-confidence that he will be able to meet life's demands. Unfortunately, school work is not considered manly. Schooling may be influential in determining what goals a person attains in later life, but it does not support the manhood image of maturing boys.

Two different writers looked at this situation, and, in different words, reached the same conclusion.

Anthony Storr quotes Clara Thompson, an American analyst, in his book, *Human Aggression*. "Aggression is not necessarily destructive at all. It springs from an innate tendency to grow and master life which seems to be characteristic of all living matter. Only when this life force is obstructed in its development do ingredients of anger, rage or hate become connected with it."

After quoting Miss Thompson, Storr goes on to formulate his own theories which seem pertinent to our held-back generation. "The more a person remains dependent on others, the more aggression will be latent within him. To be dependent on another person is to be in the power of that person." Then further on, he states, ". . . aggressive drive will be particularly marked in a species in which the young are dependent for an unusually protracted period."

Further indications why so many of our teen-agers seem to be filled with an anger that vents itself in vandalism are found in Edward V. Stein's *The Stranger Inside You*. He deduced that life has many built-in releases for "accumulative aggression." Three of them are creative work, sexual love, and play. "It is no accident that violent, destructive people always are people who (if not crippled by disease of the brain or the nervous system) are individuals who have not developed the capacity to channel the aggressive vitalities of their being into one or all three of these forms of behavior."

What are the opportunities in our society for a teen-ager to direct his energies into the three areas cited by Stein?

Creative work for a young person does not exist. Youngsters are hired to guide power lawn mowers or deliver packages or are employed in minor household repairs, but rarely are they allowed to do anything beside menial jobs. Unless a young person is inspired by an original idea to market some service or object he has produced, creativity does not characterize teen-age, money-making opportunities. Paul

Goodman made his readers aware of this problem in *Growing Up Absurd*. ". . . by and large our economic society is not geared for the cultivation of its young or the attainment of important goals that they can work toward."

The second release to alleviate the pressure of building aggression is also obstructed. Our moral code is undergoing a definite change for the college-age person. Ten years ago, the idea of persons spending the night in the dormitories of friends of the opposite sex would have been shocking. Now it is standard policy in many universities. Society, however, still seeks to persuade teen-agers to deny their growing sexuality, even though mothers in New York City and Chicago and Los Angeles may accompany their daughters to the doctors to be certain that the girl has a supply of birth control pills. The grownups have a double standard. They want the girl to have the pill but they would never admit to their friends and neighbors that it is necessary for their teen-age daughter to use the preventative. Probably the mothers say something like, "Now here are the pills, but you just make sure that you never need to take them."

Therefore the only acceptable avenue for youthful aggression is play. Adults and many teen-agers understand this. A driving vitality is very desirable in sports, as witnessed by the large cheering audience of adults which usually attends high school games. "Football and basketball provide almost the only occasion in American life when adults can empathize with and take pride in the qualities of youth with a minimum of guilt or envy. If this opportunity is frequently exploited to serve viciously competitive ends, it is also frequently the occasion for a real appreciation and affection for the young, in response to what they are actually like," wrote Edgar Z. Friedenberg in *Coming of Age in America*.

When the juvenile delinquency rate rises, recreation facilities seem an obvious answer. Policemen, with the utmost sincerity, work with the Police Athletic League (PAL), hoping to keep youngsters out of trouble by providing sports activities for them. PAL is very effective with pre-adolescents. Not all teen-age boys, however, are interested in participating in supervised sports. A favorite activity for the older age group is constructing motorized vehicles. Involved technical skills and much creative energy is used to adapt mechanisms such as lawn mower engines into motor bikes. Here is an achievement that is both creative and manly. But after days of sweat and struggle, the boys find that it is illegal to operate such devices on the street. If more communities appreciated this problem, they might provide a relatively inexpensive dirt track for the boys to test out and enjoy their creations. If there is no

available land in a suburban tract, then arrangements might be made with the owners of large shopping centers to use the empty parking lots on Sundays.

So unless a boy wants to play a game, there is
little opportunity to discharge his pent-up aggression,
which then builds higher and higher. When the
first two escape hatches are sealed, and the third
seems to lead nowhere, an incident such as happened
in New Haven, Connecticut, becomes more compre-
hensible. Several teen-age boys went to a private
community beach area one summer night. They
spilled the contents of the litter baskets all about the
sandy stretch and shoved picnic tables into the
water, riding them like rafts. The police apprehended the vandals and brought them to the local
station house.

"The boys don't drink beer or anything like that,"
said a father about his son and the boy's friends.
"They don't even smoke. They are good scholars.
How could they have gotten in such a mess?"

The answer came from one youth. "I guess you
might say we were all mad at something."

An editorial in the Hartford, Connecticut, *Courant*
a month later pondered the increase in vandalism.
"A good part of the trend seems to flow from a kind
of vengefulness. . . ." The description would fit a
young suspect arrested in Washington, D.C., a few

years ago. His crime: vandalizing works of art. Using a pair of sewing scissors, he slashed a mural depicting the signing of the Constitution and mutilated three oil portraits in the House wing of the Capitol. He was described as "mad at the world."

In *Growing Up Absurd* Paul Goodman wrote: "If they [teen-age boys] have been kept from constructive activity making them feel worthwhile, part of their energy might be envious and malicious destructiveness of property. As they are powerless, it is spite; and as they are humiliated, it is vengeance."

Recently many college-age young people have been involved in protests against the Vietnam war, racial inequalities, and the policies of their educational institutions. High school students, too, have engaged more and more frequently in demonstrations, partly as an expression of legitimate grievances, partly as a release for their contained aggression. Frequently sit-ins or picketing of school buildings turn disorderly and damage is done to furniture or to personal faculty files in no way connected with the cause. Not to be overlooked are the terrorist tactics of certain radical groups who feel bombings and arson are justified as part of their protest against the corporate, military, and educational power structures. One can only surmise that the pent-up anger and frustration of these individuals lead them beyond the bounds of legal protest.

So for many of the seemingly unmotivated acts of vandalism, the cause may be less obvious and more pervasive than is normally thought. There are, however, acts of angry vandalism which at first glance seem to be clearly motivated.

SWASTIKAS PAINTED ON LI MAN'S HOUSE
—*Newsday*

VANDALS DESECRATE 2 GREEK CHURCHES
—*New York Times*

ANOTHER SYNAGOGUE BURNS;
4 BOYS ARRESTED
—*Daily News*

The reason for vandalism in religious buildings, however, may actually be twofold. Attacks on churches and particularly synagogues seem to come in waves, initiated by the first publicized incident. The implication is clear. Some vandals are inadvertently given direction by the news media. The same boy who painted a swastika on a synagogue after hearing about a similar incident on a TV newscast might have with equal zeal sliced the tires of twenty-five parked cars or smashed the sinks in a national park men's room. Accessibility and inspiration were the determining factors. It is difficult to prove this as vandals rarely make statements about the crime for which they are charged. Often vandalism of a house of worship is no differently motivated than other acts of vandalism—an angry individual blindly striking out.

In those cases where vandals purposely seek out a certain temple or church in order to get back at a special religion, another problem must be faced. Religious and racial hatred start in the home and are reinforced by the community. Many children first hear words like "nigger" or slurring jokes about Jews and other nationality groups in their own living room.

School board and school bond programs are influenced by racial or religious feelings. In the late nineteen-sixties many districts attempted to organize visiting school programs so that students from all-white areas could meet black contemporaries. These children often had a mistaken image of black people formed by sensational newspaper and TV reports. Unfortunately, residents of white neighborhoods raised such a fuss that the interschool visits were discontinued. Issues such as the above are discussed at the dinner table or on street corners while mothers wait for the school bus with their small children. The youngsters of a community hear these conversations and are affected.

Consider a certain suburb of Los Angeles where the residential areas are unofficially segregated. There is a Jewish section, a Gentile section, and, recently, a rapidly growing Spanish-American population. Each group has its own political candidates, its own goals. One Saturday night vandals desecrated a synagogue by painting the walls with ethnic slurs, swastikas, and obscenities. The holy Torah scroll was unrolled and sprayed with a fire extinguisher. Damage was estimated at more than $10,000. Police were able to apprehend the two 15-year-old boys responsible for the wreckage because the youths had been boasting about the incident around their school. Under the provisions of the laws, the boys' names were not released. These criminals were a product of an environment where community issues are decided on a racial or religious basis.

Another example of vandalism motivated by milieu was seen when riots swept the country's black ghettos in the late nineteen-sixties. Young blacks burned and looted many square blocks of their slum districts. Just as Dallas once meant ten gallon hats and oil rigs to most people and now is synonymous with death engendered in a manic climate, Detroit once was automobiles or Motown music and now summons to mind images of sniper rifle shots and burnt-out buildings. Even the White House seemed to have been stained by the smoke of the flaming Washington slums.

This type of vandalism is similar to what in Chapter Two was labeled Positive Violence or violence

61

connected with constructive drives. In this case: the civil rights movement. An unemotional comparison between the "Indians" of the Boston Tea Party and the young blacks smashing the windows of businesses they thought belonged to nonblacks would reveal an anger about oppression. One group was being mistreated by a nation across the sea, and the second by whites living on the other side of town. Both acts had a similar effect. The dumping of tea in Boston Harbor indicated the colonists' unhappiness about taxes. The ghetto violence made a country sharply aware of the blacks' determination to get the freedom they had wanted—and had been promised—for so long.

The National Advisory Commission on Civil Disorders was formed in the summer of 1967 and investigated twenty-four disorders in twenty-three cities. The Commission found that:

> The typical rioter was a teenager or young adult, a lifelong resident of the city in which he rioted, a high school dropout; he was, nevertheless, somewhat better educated than his non-rioting Negro neighbor and was usually underemployed or employed in a menial job. He was proud of his race, extremely hostile to both whites and middle class Negroes and although informed about politics highly distrustful of the political system.

The cause of the anger which prompted these widespread acts of vandalism was multifaceted: lack of employment, mistreatment by authorities, resentment at inequality, and incitement by militant leaders. By the summer of 1969, however, the major disturbances appeared to have ceased with only sporadic flare-ups. That August, the *New York Times* headlined, "U.S. OFFICIALS SAY BIG RIOTS ARE OVER." The article explained, "There are a number of reasons for the decline in the big city riots, but the major one seems to be that the militant Negro leaders are now counseling against violence that destroys the neighborhood in which the blacks live."

Whether this form of ghetto-inspired vandalism has really died out or not, public officials should not be lulled into complacency. The needs of our black citizens are still to be met; the causes behind their resentment still exist.

Though large-scale vandalism is not as prevalent in ghettos, the less noticeable variety is still present. In *all* economic areas the problem of wrecked empty buildings is a big one.

"A vacant house is just like an open invitation to become a vandal," a member of the Nassau County Police Department said. "Don't move out until the new owners take over. They'll [vandals] destroy it. Just destroy it."

In suburban areas this trouble is not as deadly as

in slums. If an empty store or a model house for a housing development is vacant for any amount of time, the windows are usually broken. So all the entrances into the structure are boarded up. Shingles are then sometimes cracked or walls are smeared with obscenities. Once this happens, neighbors or nearby business people complain to the town and the delinquent owner is forced to remove the unsightly damage or markings. Thus the situation is eradicated because the people living in the area are the property owners.

In ghettos, however, the landlords are difficult to find and when they *are* located, they usually have no desire to invest more money into something that is not bringing in sufficient financial rewards. Soon the vandalized hulks attract drug addicts, drunks, and teen-agers anxious to be unobserved. All too often the final step in the degradation is fire. Someone deliberately puts a match to the crumbling mass. In the past, addicts sleeping off a dose of narcotics have been trapped and fatally burned. The plight of the residents does not seem to motivate the slumlords to curb the problem.

A hopeful trend is beginning to develop though. More ghetto inhabitants are banding together and putting pressure on city governments to force the absentee owners to improve the situation. There are uses to which the more easily salvaged buildings might be put.

Angry Vandalism

The Harlem Addicts Rehabilitation Center has begged politicians to help them find an additional center. The present facility turns away forty-five teen-agers a week, forty-five young people desperately seeking help for their drug problem. A mother of a 15-year-old heroin addict told the *Daily News*, "There are plenty of vacant buildings around where kids have been found dead. Why can't we get one where we can teach them to live?"

Community leaders would be wise to appreciate the fact that angry vandalism stems from many causes: subtle and overt, psychological and sociological. All too often easy remedies such as recreation centers or sports nights at the local high school seem a solution, and all too often these fail. Totally different ways of fighting vandalism may have to be originated if the crime seems motivated by anger. Possibly clinics to help parents understand the drives and needs of their teen-age children or intensive education campaigns to alert the residents to the dangers of racial or religious bitterness.

Angry vandalism is often the easiest of the three types of vandalism to identify and the most difficult to eradicate.

6

Community Reaction

"And just like you I sit and wonder why"
—Roger & Roger

Vandalism is a crime of darkness, light being an effective foe. Usually the destruction is committed at night and not discovered until the following day. Events too late for the morning edition of the newspaper make exciting early newscasts.

"Lexington Senior High School was hit by vandals in the early hours of this morning. The cost of the fire is placed at one hundred thousand dollars."

Once released, the news gives birth to rumors, anger, and amazement which coil higher and higher, encircling—

Vandalism

THE HIGH SCHOOL GIRLS set free for the day with a liberty tinged by a vague guilt: "Isn't it awful? Miss Erinson's room was all burned out. Someone said we won't have Home Ec for the rest of the year."

THE CHIEF OF THE ARSON SQUAD picking his way over the fallen ceiling tiles in the school corridor and entering the chemistry lab: "Just like that other school fire two months ago. They lit those books and papers, turned on the gas jets, and got out before they were blown to hell."

THE BOARD OF EDUCATION PRESIDENT buzzing his secretary: "Notify all board members there's a special meeting tonight. We have to find better security measures for the buildings and grounds in this district."

TWO BOYS, sitting on the hood of an old Chevy at the hamburger stand: "Crap! How much you wanna bet we go on split session, and I end up in the afternoon. Just what I need. To get outta school six-thirty every day!"

And later that afternoon the newspapers are delivered to the front doors. Maybe there is a picture on the fourth or fifth page, showing the charred science room or a shot of the high school principal sadly surveying the damage. Within a few days, however, more outspoken reactions appear in print:

Is there no one in all our vast school system who can at least make some attempt to protect our school system from these lowly firebugs and vandals?
—a letter to the editor
Los Angeles Times

Respect for property is a trait which must be taught beginning with a child's very earliest years in the home. . . . One of the most positive steps needed in the prevention of vandalism is reasonable and closer supervision by parents.
—article
Insight

And one that makes everybody nod and wish that the pen was really mightier than the vandal's match:

The community may not have all the answers and it has to cope with a larger world where vandalism is commonplace. . . . One thing is certain, however. We are going to keep on talking and meeting and trying and we are going to succeed.
—editorial
The Massapequa Post

If the town is near a larger city, the school fire may even deserve a mention on TV with a few feet of film rolling while the commentator ties this act of vandalism to what other villages and cities have suffered. Possibly the school superintendent or a community leader will be briefly interviewed and asked what they intend to do.

Often the answer is, "Educate the community to the seriousness of the problem." The idea is wise, but the problem of inertia is met everywhere. A Long Island school district with 16,744 students held a well-advertised panel discussion for parents, entitled "Vandalism in Our Schools" in November. Eighteen people were in the audience.

Less than two months later vandals set a $50,000 fire in the high school. One month after the night of destruction, a civic association sent leaflets to all residents, pleading for them to come to a meeting to organize a fight against vandalism. The meeting was poorly attended, the fight never fought.

Panel discussions whether on vandalism or narcotics rarely attract a large audience. Yet policemen constantly hear from parents, "But how was I supposed to know my child was using narcotics?" Or— "Breaking windows? Are you sure it's *my* son? He said something about going to the movies tonight." Ironically, the few people who do attend public discussion sessions on youth problems are often aware of the situation already. Their children are less likely to be the ones involved in the illegal activities.

So the first wave of explosive reactions crests and crashes, receding with a soft hissing noise. The tellings and retellings have worn out the story with overuse.

Now begin the quieter reactions.

SCHOOLS

Schools have a special share of the burden in the fight against vandalism because educational buildings seem to be the main target of vandals. Sometimes the vandalism is the result of anger at school officials. Other incidents might just be children striking out in a setting where they spend much of their time. Appreciating these facts, educators can evolve successful ways to eliminate vandalism by attacking its core.

In the January 1970 *The Instructor,* an article entitled "Can We Lessen Vandalism?" stated that "the teacher's first tool is class discussion." Writer Raymond Greenstein went on to say, "If the discussion is on a permissive, low-pressure level, reasons for vandalism such as mischief, thoughtlessness, resentment, maladjustment, and rebellion against authority emerge." Once the reasons have been verbalized, teachers can use a variety of methods to instruct the children.

A change in the philosophy or staff of the institutions might be necessary in certain cases. Nathan Goldman prepared a socio-psychological study of school vandalism, based on his evaluation of sixteen junior high, junior-senior high, and all senior high schools of Syracuse, New York. "A low level of personal identification with the school and its goals among students, teachers, and parents was found positively associated with a high rate of vandalic behavior among students," wrote Mr. Goldman. "High damage schools, also, were found characterized by inadequate administration and leadership, with poor communication among the various members of the school."

Consider also the effect on children of parents who constantly complain about school taxes or teachers or district policies. If the adults appear to have no respect for the educational system, why should the children?

So if certain buildings in a district suffer more vandalism than others, a little soul searching on the part of the staff and community might be in order.

School districts with excessive vandalism have sought other methods to combat youthful lawbreakers. The use of tough plastic panes rather than glass in school windows has been very successful in Milwaukee, Phoenix, and Kansas City, Missouri. Some systems have purchased electronic warning devices such as alarms that can be triggered by an unusual noise. The last custodian to leave at night sets the main switch so that if any forced entry or other damage is done, the alarm will detect the sound and ring. Though there have been instances where a noisy heating system has activated the alarm, school districts have apprehended window breakers and burglars with the help of these surveillance mechanisms.

A highly effective though controversial preventive is the use of trained dogs roaming the building at night. The animals have access to all rooms and have been trained to accept no food. Several times a night a handler will take the dogs outside for fresh air. Though department stores have used such dogs for years, many parents object when their district contemplates employing them. Perhaps these people do not realize that the dogs only attack when the intruder attempts to escape, otherwise the animals are trained to hold the person at bay. The advantage of having the dogs can not be denied. For example, Brentwood School District, New York, reported that dogs had reduced vandalism by almost 100 percent.

Though the cost varies with the rental agency, the price is actually less than security guards who are not as effective. On a six-month basis the estimated cost to one East Coast school district was approximately $8,000 compared with $19,000 for security guards. With the acknowledged success of the dogs, more and more troubled school districts can be expected to employ them.

Schools are morally obligated to educate the children and their parents to the causes and extent of the local vandalism. At the same time precautionary measures have to be investigated to protect the buildings. But these devices do not change the situation. They only provide defense while the problem is attacked.

YOUTH COMMISSIONS

A youth commission or youth board or youth task force is a committee appointed to "stop the outbreak of vandalism" or halt the "rising crime rate among our young people." The technique is an excellent one that ought to produce notable results. There is a built-in, "self-destruct" quality, however, which often negates the commission's effectiveness. The flaw is generally in its membership, which like the characters in old-fashioned melodramas is consistent from town to city.

    A. An elected official named to the head position by an elected official
    B. A school superintendent
    C. A PTA president

D. A businessman to represent the local trades-people

E. A member of the clergy

One glance at the list and it is possible to know the tone of the commission.

The guiding hand should not be a politician because politicians never forget the voters. What would happen if the commission found the community itself was sick? Is it easy to persuade voters that the good life they are providing for their offspring is actually detrimental to the youngsters' mental and physical health? "Nothing is more common than the idea that we, the people living in the Western world of the twentieth century, are eminently sane," wrote Eric Fromm in *The Sane Society*.

It's difficult to convince *people* their way of life is wrong. It's impossible to convince *voters*.

Another type of politician in his own community is the school superintendent. His job is so immense that he can not be expected to be sensitive to the pulse of the students while keeping Board of Education members, divergent community groups, several competing unions, and his entire staff happy. His job, too, is dependent upon the temper of the people he serves.

Actually, the membership list of the commission reads like a compilation of the people who should be *interviewed* by the committee. The five types would be excellent sources when trying to determine the extent and types of vandalism being inflicted upon the community. But what is needed on the commission itself are people who appreciate the vastness of the problem and *are in touch with the young people*.

Where are these champions?

In the high school classrooms.

"No one can solve youths' problems for them. They must solve them for themselves," said Dr. William C. Kvaraceus, a well-known Boston educator.

It is inconceivable that a panel examining a serious issue involving young people does not have a teen-ager in its ranks. Teen-ager does not necessarily mean a student leader or a hard-core delinquent. With a little intelligence and a vast amount of honesty, it would be possible to involve boys usually labeled as troublemakers, those on the periphery of the courtroom society. They know what is going on in their town, and though the commission won't learn names (and it had better not even ask for them) something more valuable may be revealed. Reasons.

Senior Scholastic Magazine claimed the age range for vandals is 9 to 21, with far more boys involved than girls. These estimates are similar to those in most articles and discussions about vandalism.

Since the majority of vandals are teen-age boys, a man is needed who can deal with teen-age boys. Who knows and understands young men better than an athletic coach? There is a common misconception that coaches spend all their time explaining the ins and outs of their particular sport. More accurately, coaches are part-time psychologists, father-confessors, doctors, and arbiters. A successful coach has found the two-way highway of communication with boys. The talent ought to be utilized. A coach would be an excellent choice for a youth commission.

One of the other appointees to the commission is usually a business representative. Careful selection would provide not only a member of the tradespeople but a person who knows youngsters and their problems. Such a person was involved in a telling incident that happened on Long Island a few years ago.

The owner of a luncheonette had died. The store was a gathering place for the less-appreciated teenagers: "the town bums" (as they called themselves). A delegation of these young people appeared in the office of the local newspaper and placed a small ad, bordered in black:

"Pappa Joe" is dead. This is a great loss to the teenagers of Massapequa Park.

Joe Guercio was like a father to the kids on Park Blvd., always willing to advise them, willing to help them get jobs, and always standing by in case of trouble.

We will miss "Pappa Joe" because in these times of trouble, he always remained calm and tried to keep things under control. May he rest in peace!

THE KIDS OF MASSAPEQUA PARK
—The Massapequa Post

What influence a man like "Pappa Joe" could have wielded on the right youth commission!

So—while there are relatively successful youth commissions, more would serve their function better if the members were selected primarily for their empathy with young people.

RECREATION CENTERS

A traditional suggestion of youth commissions is that a recreation center be established. Certainly any town that is not providing such activities is remiss in its duties.

In Brookhaven, New York, twenty youths had to seize a vacant supermarket, bring in a stereo phonograph, twenty chairs, a lamp, and a wooden table before the town officials stopped talking and began doing something to establish a community center.

While the youths' illegal occupation of the building is questionable, it does implicate a neglectful town government.

During the summer of 1969, Middletown, Connecticut, suffered sporadic rumbles between black and white youths, some window smashing, and a few attempted robberies. The images of Detroit and Watts and Newark had been burned into the nation's memory, so the situation may have been viewed with more alarm than it warranted. At any rate the city had several tense days and nights. After the mood had become more relaxed, the local paper admitted that "serious discussion developed relative to the planning for a youth center for whites and blacks."

Unfortunately, crises seem to be needed to impel many towns to provide the basics of modern day living. Recreation centers, however, will not eradicate vandalism.

In one Long Island school district, gangs of fifty and sixty youths would leave their weekly Teen Night and cause considerable damage to the homes and property lining the route home. Another junior high school had to suspend their sports and dance activities because there was so much destruction to the building. The huge globe lights illuminating the front walks were removed, and games started between groups of boys, using the globes as soccer balls. The dances required plain-clothes men as guards because many youths were arriving intoxicated.

The highest incidence of vandalism in a heavily populated New York State county occurred in the community which had pools, tennis courts, playfields, and all kinds of recreational arrangements. As was shown in the previous three chapters, idleness is not always the cause of vandalism. One does wonder if the parents in this town were using the facilities the way many parents use TV: something to distract the children, to keep them occupied and "out of my hair."

A growing community must provide certain things for its residents: a safe water supply, street lights, law enforcement. Recreational facilities for young as well as old is another right to be expected by taxpayers, but these leisure activities are not the end-all of youth problems.

CURFEWS

A curfew can be viewed two ways. A vestigial solution left over from a time when the world was divided into small towns and isolated areas. Or the ultimate weapon to be employed when all semblance of control has been lost.

In today's world of sprawling suburbs where it is impossible to know where one town ends and another begins, a curfew for teen-agers would be difficult to enforce. Even if the major obstacle of arranging for neighboring towns to agree to a curfew was overcome, how would the police find enough men to patrol the area?

During the riot scare in Middletown, Connecticut, Mayor Kenneth J. Dooley of that city, imposed a 10 P.M. to 5 A.M. curfew. Both blacks and whites condemned him. *The Middletown Press* editorialized, ". . . the curfew last night, although carried out with commendable diplomacy, stretched police forces so thin that it was impossible to maintain any particular level of enforcement without resorting to mass arrests."

The imposition of a curfew involves much weighing of issues or the decision may cause a reaction worse than the original problem.

Hollywood's Sunset Strip became a battleground when the city attempted to enforce a 10 P.M. curfew. Night club and restaurant owners had demanded the curfew when unruly juvenile gangs began hurting their business. For several weekends after that, nearly a thousand youths roamed the area, hurling rocks and eggs, attacking cars, and waving protest signs.

There is something inherently debasing about a

curfew, reviving memories in those old enough to recall World War II of occupied countries and Nazi boots on dark, cobblestone streets. Legally, courts in California and Florida have declared curfew laws unconstitutional. And for younger people a curfew means a freedom hard won from parents is denied by a city.

In terms of vandalism, a curfew's success is negligible. It is a weapon for another kind of war.

Too often the various attempts by a community to solve the problem of vandalism fail through mismanagement or a lack of interest or petty politics. Added to the real menace now is the psychological fear that nothing can be done to stop it. This panic leads certain men to attempt to solve the situation by their own means.

Vigilantism.

7

Vigilantism and Auxiliary Police

"There's a man with a gun over there,
telling me I've got to beware."
                              —*Stephen Stills*

Whether we wish to admit it or not, the phenomenon of vigilantism appears to be purely American. So concluded Richard Maxwell Brown in *The History of Violence in America.* The facts substantiate his premise.

In that period of our country's history when the Western frontiers were edging toward the Pacific Ocean, effective law enforcement was rare if not totally absent. There could be only one solution. Members of the community had to combine to fight the lawless elements. In such a setting the vigilantes could be a positive force because they supplied the lacking protection. But one must realize that many innocents were undoubtedly wrongly punished by this rushed form of justice. The totally negative aspects of vigilantism were seen in these situations where the unofficial law enforcement groups formed, defeated the enemy, and then sought another foe. This is what happened after the Civil War when an agrarian United States began the metamorphosis into industrialization. The tentacles of vigilantism snaked out "to include a variety of targets connected to the tensions of the New America: Catholics, Jews, Negroes, immigrants, laboring men and labor leaders, political radicals, advocates of civil liberties, and non-conformists in general," wrote the aforementioned Mr. Brown.

Vigilantes lost their official support and went underground during the late nineteenth century. In March 1872, the *New York Times* editorialized about crime in the city, seeing vigilantism as the least desirable solution. "Must it [crime] go on with ever increasing violence, until an outraged community unable to bear it longer, shall arise and execute lawless vengeance on the criminal?"

Present-day smoldering racial tensions have produced two types of vigilantes. Whites who unite to protect themselves and their community against fear of blacks. Blacks who unite to protect themselves and their community against fear of whites. In

Crown Heights, Brooklyn, the Macabees organized and patrolled the streets. The group was mainly Hasidic Jewish in its membership of 250, although some white Christians and blacks also belonged to the Macabees. "The crime problem was mostly by teen-age Negroes coming into Crown Heights from adjacent areas. By March 1966 the *New York Times* reported that crime had fallen in the Crown Heights area and that the Macabees were patrolling at a reduced rate." So wrote Richard Maxwell Brown in *The History of Violence in America.*

Elsewhere, a group of black youths formed their own police force in Central Islip, New York, in order to protect their Soul Village Youth Center and the members of the black community. Two black teenagers had been attacked and the windows of the center had been smashed after racial incidents occurred at a nearby movie theater. The protective group patrolled on foot, carrying billy clubs because they felt the blacks did not get sufficient police protection from whites.

Vandalism, too, has begot vigilantes.

About forty persons formed an organization in the Plainedge School District, New York, following a wave of destructive acts by high school youngsters. The vandalism culminated late one Friday night when house and automobile windows were smashed by bricks, a car radio antenna speared a living room

87

window, and a Volkswagen was overturned. Thereafter men patrolled the residential blocks on foot and in cars. If trouble broke out, a whistle shriek assembled the whole group in a few minutes.

"We don't need this," said a spokesman of the local police precinct.

Certain people in Plainedge felt otherwise.

"All the neighbors are cooperating in the general area," a member of the group told a local paper. "I just sit in the bushes and wait. I'm looking to protect my property and I'll use anything of mine to protect it, including my two fists. I can't leave my wife and children home alone without worrying about them."

One individual confronted by the Plainedge minutemen had a chance to describe his experience. On Friday nights, 17-year-old Frank M. usually visited his girl friend whose mother worked evenings. In order to avoid a pesty neighbor who in the past had told the girl's mother imaginative tales about what supposedly went on when the two young people were alone, Frank decided to make a discreet arrival.

"So I cut through a couple yards, you know, and went to the back door. And then wham! Guys came running from everywhere with flashlights and baseball bats, yelling and carrying on like hell! All I could think about was that old woman next door and what she was gonna tell my girl's mother."

The incident seems similar to another confrontation between vigilantes and their supposed enemy.

A group of local residents in Lake Grove, New York, were disturbed by a rash of teen-age vandalism which they felt the local police were not able to halt.

One member, who would not give his name to a local paper for fear of reprisals from the vandals, said, "We've had at least 100 acts of vandalism in the past year, from setting redwood lawn furniture on fire to destroying mailboxes."

One night the Lake Grove police received a call about eleven o'clock. A large unruly group had congregated in the area. Two patrol cars were dispatched to investigate the situation. The officers arrived to find a car with several teen-aged occupants surrounded by a mob of 30 vigilantes. The police released the car and ordered the vigilantes to disperse.

Fortunately for all concerned, these incidents ended without injury to innocent persons. The danger of an over-zealous vigilante, however, is not to be minimized. In Cairo, Illinois, a Negro boy was shot in the leg. Black leaders suggested it was the work of white vigilantes, four of whom were supposedly spotted driving a 1962 blue Chevy in the area shortly before the youth was shot. During a 1968 disturbance in Cleveland, Ohio, two Negro men were shot far from the city violence but in an area where white vigilantes were active.

This is the inherent danger of vigilantism. Not

only can these groups cause additional problems as the police in Lake Grove learned, but no matter how strong the leadership, vigilantes border on mob rule. Policemen operate under a very tight code of laws for the obvious reason that a sense of power can affect a person's behavior. Vigilantes are to be feared for the lack of proper controls. There is an organization, however, which has the full sanction of the legal law enforcement agencies, even though its members are volunteers. The Civil Defense Auxiliary Police.

"Auxiliary police units? They're good. Some of them are very excellent," a spokesman for the Nassau County Police Department said recently.

In the adjoining county of Suffolk, a detective with the Juvenile Aid Bureau nodded emphatically when asked if he approved of auxiliary police. "I don't know why those guys do it. But thank God they do. They help with traffic on Sundays. Some patrol their towns at night. And you know they pay for their own uniforms right out of their own pockets. And when you do that you're talking about a hundred and fifty dollars."

Nassau County Civil Defense Auxiliary Police receive some money from the county government for uniforms and equipment. Nothing goes for salaries because everyone is a volunteer. Some units such as Auxiliary Police Unit 315 get their funds from village taxes because they are in an incorporated vil-age.

"The community has been very helpful," George R. Collins, chief of Unit 315, explained one night as he readied the car for patrol. "Besides this car, we have three station wagons at our disposal if we need them."

Chief Collins checked the Civilian Band radio which connected to the dispatcher at headquarters. In addition the automobile carried a walkie-talkie and an FM radio set that could, also, call the dispatcher.

"There. We're all set," the officer said.

With the temperature hovering at freezing, the 1969 white station wagon, gold letters glittering on the front doors, pulled away from the old brick house which served as headquarters. Chief Collins would drive this "run." A younger patrolman named Bob sat on the passenger side. He gripped his night-stick, which is lighter than it appears but as "good as a gun in some cases." Auxiliary policemen carry no firearms.

The blue uniforms are exactly like those of the official police except for triangular orange patches on both arms. These emblems testify that the man has successfully completed a 13-week course super-vised by the NCPD. The men study fingerprinting, traffic control, first aid, laws of arrest, defensive tactics, plus other subjects similar to those mastered by the regular police.

"We're going to check out the park first tonight." Chief Collins unhooked the CB microphone from the dashboard. "Headquarters. One-oh-one."

101 is the code number of the patrol car.

Almost immediately came, "This is Headquarters. Go ahead, one-oh-one."

"Entering post eight-nine from the south."

"Right, one-oh-one."

"One-oh-one, clear."

"Headquarters, clear."

The car swung onto a wide dirt trail that followed a twisting stream through a two-mile length of woods. The state park several years before had not been safe after dark. An attempted rape, muggings, and gang beatings had taken place there. Houses bordering the wooded strip had been burglarized, many homes more than once. A common complaint on summer weekends was that 14- and 15-year-olds were running through the backyards at three and four o'clock in the morning.

"Since we cleaned it out," Chief Collins said simply, "anyone can walk there day or night."

What he did not describe was how the families along the park edge were truly thankful for the effectiveness of the auxiliary police. One resident had been ready to sell his house before the nightly patrols had been initiated.

The car slowed to a 10-mile-per-hour crawl, and both men eyed the woods and trails. Bob rolled down his window and lifted out a sealed beam spotlight which resembled a photographer's flash gun. Holding it above the car roof, he flicked the switch. The beam illuminated the far side of a reservoir—a distance of one thousand feet. Edge-of-the-seat alert, the men scanned the brown, grassy shore and the wall of leafless trees. Conversation had ceased and only the rumbling car motor and the squawking of disturbed ducks broke the cold silence.

The distant shore converged with the nearer shore, and the car picked up speed. The men sat back, more relaxed.

"This is the place where we still have trouble with beer parties in the summer." Chief Collins pointed to the far side of the stream: a mass of bramble and bushes. "The kids stand in there and taunt us. Call us rent-a-cops. Some of our younger men go after them, but I don't encourage it."

Though Bob said nothing, his soft laughter at the particular moment hinted much.

The north entrance of the park was picked up by the car headlights. Chief Collins radioed headquarters: "Leaving post eight-nine from the north. All clear."

From there One-Hundred-One checked a junior high school and two elementary schools. At each post the car slowed, and the powerful beam illuminated the windows and doors to make sure there had been no illegal entries. Should the men have found anything suspicious, the official police would have been called immediately.

Auxiliary policemen are well aware that they are only *auxiliary* policemen and do not try to usurp powers that are denied them. If a patrolman should arrive on an accident scene, he would first notify the regular police and take control until the official squad car arrived. Auxiliary policemen are permitted to make a Civilian Arrest like any other citizen. This means "for an offense committed or attempted in his presence" or "when the person arrested has committed a felony although not in his presence."

As the patrol car approached the high school, Chief Collins' glance evaluated a potential problem. The school was having an art and music festival that evening. The parking lot was jammed.

"We might have to come back and help with the traffic here," he said thoughtfully.

This time when he radioed headquarters, the report was "Activity."

Seemingly, before the word was spoken, the dispatcher fired back, "Right, one-oh-one."

After the report had been completed, Chief Collins settled back for the mile and a half drive to the library, the next post to be checked.

"You've got to hand it to those dispatchers. Those

kids are really on their toes. And they're only 17 years old. Too young to join as patrolmen. But they're sharp all right."

Each night from about seven to eleven-thirty or until the last run is completed, the boys tend the headquarters' radio. They volunteer their time and usually arrive at their post with a stack of high school texts so they can complete their homework. In addition to maintaining contact with the patrol car, they monitor a police radio which receives messages transmitted to official police cars. Stolen car reports are given on this radio, and the boys of Unit 315 when off duty have been responsible for spotting several stolen cars and reporting them to the NCPD.

"You would have been proud of these dispatchers last winter," the chief continued, a paternal pride coloring his voice. "During that big snowstorm they stuck to their post for thirty-six hours straight, telling us about stalled cars or who needed a nurse or where milk should be delivered. We're all mighty proud of them."

The public library—post nine-two—occupied a well-lighted corner near a large shopping center. Yet the two men approached the area with caution. Bob, nightstick in hand, went down an outside flight of steps to inspect the back door. Chief Collins sat in the idling car, eyes trained on the stairway.

"We give a patrolman a few minutes," he said.

"Then if they don't come back, we go after them. No telling who could be waiting down there."

In a few moments Bob reappeared. After a close check of all windows and doors, the auxiliary policemen headed for a church that had been vandalized several times by youngsters of the area. Next One-Hundred-One went to the fire department which had requested that the building be included in the nightly tour because children often stoned the windows. The first run ended at the Village Hall, an hour and forty-seven minutes after it had started. In the garage area, Chief Collins proudly showed off "Big Moe," which is the rescue truck equipped with an aluminum boat and every kind of tool needed for an emergency.

During a 20-minute coffee break back at headquarters, the chief had time to answer some questions about the auxiliary police.

Who is qualified to join?

"Any U.S. citizen, male, 21. He has to live in the community and be able to pass an investigation by the county police and the FBI."

Why do men become auxiliary policemen?

"That's hard to say. Some men just want to be a part of something. They can't do anything about the big problems of the country, but they *can* do something about crime in their own town. Other times our dispatchers join when they become 21. One man

I heard of joined another unit because the patrolmen found his teen-age son drunk by the side of the road one night and brought the boy home before something serious happened to him. The father was so grateful that he joined the unit and is one of their most loyal men."

The rest and question period were interrupted by an alert on the police radio. There had been a robbery several blocks from the park, post eight-nine. The thief was armed with a Luger and had three hundred dollars in cash and another hundred in checks. So as Bob slid behind the wheel for the second run of the night, there was added tension. It heightened as the car swung back onto the trail through the state park. The dark woods might be concealing a nervous man clutching a loaded gun.

"All we have to do is spot him," Chief Collins said. "We wouldn't go after him, of course. But just seeing him would be a tremendous help to the police."

The dispatcher kept One-Hundred-One informed about the robbery. The suspect had driven off after committing the crime. Still Bob and Chief Collins didn't relax even when driving from one post to another. By the sheerest bit of luck, they might spot the car.

The tour was uneventful: no robbery suspect, no vandals. If a man is hunting for a thrilling, adventure-packed evening, he should go to the movies and not the auxiliary police. Being a volunteer patrolman is a serious and often a routine job, but a vital contribution to the community.

"If you could count the dollars and cents value of our uniforms in terms of cutting down vandalism, you'd be amazed," Chief Collins said as the car cruised around East Lake Elementary School. "Do you know that for the last three years—since we've been patrolling—there has been no act of destruction on Halloween to any of our schools. That's something to think about."

8

Peer Reaction

"Oh, Mother, tell your children
Not to do what I have done."
                    —*Alan Price*

Two things are evident when discussing vandalism
with young people. The first is immediately obvious.
Their reactions are in most cases similar to those of
adults. Whether they have inherited these attitudes
from the grownups or if reactions are reactions no
matter what age, it is difficult to tell.

"I can't stand it," said a 15-year-old Plainview,
New York, girl when asked about the defaced walls
of her high school girls' room. "I complained about
it in my Health Class." Her philosophy of action
seems to duplicate that of those adults who feel no
matter what the problem, there is an authority to
whom they can complain.

One can hear the echo of grumbling adults in the

words of a 17-year-old suburban boy who was referring to school vandalism when he told an interviewer, "I don't know. I don't like it. I think it's kind of . . . I think it's pretty bad. It kind of shows that kids have nothing else to do. Instead of doing something constructive, you do something destructive. That's what's kind of sad really."

The second thing that might happen when a person listens to accounts by teen-agers is that the vandalistic acts become more understandable. No longer do vandals seem like horrible villains who create the astronomical destruction costs, but merely everyday youngsters reacting to the influences that have formed them.

A 16-year-old boy from a middle-class suburb: "Walk into my room. It's full of street signs. Last year I wanted street signs. I got most of them as gifts. Birthdays, kids would walk in with signs. You don't know they're signs. They're covered with newspapers. Rip the newspaper off. It says, 'Detour.' And for Christmas you find one under the tree or if one's hanging loose off a signpost, you can't resist it. You rip it off, you bring it home, and you put it on the wall."

A person would feel foolish quoting to this good-natured boy figures such as the annual $100,000 cost of replacing road signs to the state of Oregon Highway Department. Yet the figures exist, and the bills must be paid by taxes.

Many parents agree that individual vandals might conceivably be their children; those that do minor crimes such as painting stop signs to read Don't Stop. But such parents generally believe that the damage-doers causing the costly wreckage must come from other families. Their offspring could not be responsible for what they read in *Time*. "The U.S. Office of Education in Washington sets the annual cost of destruction in public schools alone at more than $100 million." Yet the nicest, most everyday teen-agers appear to have a side the parents know nothing about.

A girl, 15 years old, from Westbury, New York: "When I was small . . . well, like when I was in elementary school, I must say I was destructive. I really was. We thought it was fun just to break bottles. Coke bottles. It's mostly the kids in the elementary school [who do the damage to schools]. The older you get, the more you really feel bad about it . . . like how much the broken windows cost. The kids that are now in elementary school don't realize that their parents pay for it. For kicks they break windows. They think it's really great, you know. It isn't kids from the high school who break the [high school] windows, it's the younger kids who come around the high school."

A 17-year-old boy in the same group agreed. "It's like fun to do something bad. Like when you break a window. At first you're scared. And when you run off, you laugh and everything. It's really fun."

An interviewer asked, "Do you mean being scared is kind of fun?"

"That's probably it. It's just fun doing something wrong. When I was a little older, I didn't like to break things as much or . . . there's like more awareness. I don't know what you call it."

The above comments were by youngsters who were in no way malicious individuals, youngsters a person would want his own child to be like, but teen-agers who had nevertheless gone through a vandalistic stage. This may be another reason why the crime is widespread and hard to eliminate. Vandalism has become part of a child's emotional growth. The blame for this fact can only be placed on the adult world. Some people agree with this, ridding themselves of guilt by blaming "this permissive society" we live in. Paul Goodman in *Growing Up Absurd* defends raising children permissively but indicates the place where the fault lies: "Where upbringing is permissive, it is necessary to have strong values and esteemed behavior at home and in the community, so that the child can have worthwhile goals to structure his experience; and, of course, it is just these that are lacking."

Not only do vandals become more human when a person talks with young people, but what the teen-agers say seems to back up the psychological theories concerning the problem.

EROSIVE VANDALISM: "Destroying things is wrong," stated a 15-year-old suburban girl. "Writing on walls is all right. Walls can be washed." After a moment's reflection, she added, "Sometimes signs cause damage. Like 'Keep Off the Grass.' So you walk on the grass. Teen-agers just want to do the opposite of the sign."

FUN VANDALISM: A 16-year-old boy: "Junior high! Those are your fun years. Really. Seventh, Eighth, Ninth grades. You go out, break windows, steal bicycle tires while the rest of the bicycle is chained to the rack, and when construction crews come around you let the air out of the big tires overnight, and they have to pump it up in the morning and they never get anything done. This is mostly in junior high. Then in high school it all simmers down. Someone comes up and says, 'Hey, you want to go out bustin' windows tonight?' You say, 'Get off the wall!' "

ANGRY VANDALISM: A dialogue between four teen-agers and an adult interviewer produced a feeling about why some youngsters are angry.

A 15-year-old city boy described his pre-teen years: "It's kind of crowded where we live and there are all apartment houses, you know. And down at one end of the block we used to play stick ball, punch ball, and all that stuff. And there was a church across the street. That was like a home run. If you hit it that's a home run. Nobody ever came out and bothered us about that but I lived in a Polish section. They used to stick their heads out the window. Hot boiling pots of water, they used to chuck at us and start yelling at us, curse in Polish and all. I had a Polish friend and he knew them [the Polish curse words]. This one lady had a parrot that she trained to say cute words. She used to keep it out on the fire escape."

The boy's 16-year old suburban friend added his ideas: "Most of the time old people never tell you why they don't want you doing it, why they don't want you playing there. They just tell you don't do it. If you ask them why, they think you're getting fresh, wising off, and [they] go and tell your mother. And my mother and father they don't want to know why either. They just say, 'Get lost. Don't play there any more.'"

"Maybe you're not speaking to them as politely as you think you are," suggested the interviewer.

A 15-year-old girl tried to explain the problem more clearly. "Well, sometimes it gets to a point . . . like . . . you try to explain. And they don't let you. And you get madder and madder. And you start yelling at them. Because I know that happens with my mother. If something goes wrong and I try to explain to my mother . . . if she's mad at me she just yells and she doesn't let me explain. And I start yelling and my father gets aggravated because I'm yelling at my mother. . . ."

The fourth boy, a 15-year-old, said, "That's why our big thing is egg throwing or tomato throwing. We used to pick people. Different days we used to hit different people. Cause, you know, it kept bugging us about not playing in the street if the ball goes on their lawn and stuff so we just pick them one night and the next night another person. I mean . . . if they asked you to move down, I mean we could maybe move down for them . . . so anyway . . . they usually don't ask you to move . . . they just tell you don't play there any more."

Teen-agers seem to have so much self-awareness about their part in the vandalism problem that the next question they are asked is almost inevitable.

"What can we do to stop vandalism?" an interviewer asks.

The conversation halts.

"What *can* you do?" asked the 15-year-old girl.

The others study their shoes or their fingernails or shrug. Or else they stare at the interviewer as if he is a little peculiar to ask such a question. Perhaps they are right. Persons expecting easy answers ought to ask easy questions.

A partial answer may be the now-beginning movement to use young people to combat vandalism. *Senior Scholastic* published an article entitled "Wreckreation," which suggested, "Vandalism is a teen-age problem. Teen-agers might be just the people to come up with a creative and just solution." The article raised the possibility that teen-agers might set up groups or programs to investigate the cause of vandalism in their towns.

The suggestion bears consideration. Certainly, teen-agers talk most frankly with other teen-agers. Some communities have re-instituted town hall "gripe" sessions in order to give the adult citizens an opportunity to set forth their complaints and at the same time to allow the elected officials to keep their fingers on the pulse of the village. How about "rap" sessions where young people could talk freely? One East Coast community tried this and while the discussions went well, there was another difficulty. "Parents were the problem," said a student. "They were lined up on the streets [outside the meeting] everyone on different sides, over-reacting. No one wanted to hear the truth." So at these "rap" sessions teen-agers should speak not to adults who tend to get emotional when confronted with forthright teen-agers, but to fellow teen-agers who would have some influence to change the disturbing conditions.

Not to be discounted is the trend toward lowering the voting age. With younger voters there will be younger people elected. This situation would certainly help in the fight against vandalism. There would be more people who understood the causes of the crime in positions where they could effect changes.

There are other ideas for using young people to fight vandalism. For instance, a letter to the editor of the *Los Angeles Times*:

> Set up honor guards to patrol the schools, consisting of students who live in the immediate vicinity, who could take turns patrolling the school properties, for short daylight periods, when the buildings were unoccupied.

Almost in reply—though in no way influenced by the letter—was the decision of the Town of Huntington, New York, to request $63,200 of state funds to set up a town youth patrol which would be an adjunct to the regular police force. The idea is much like the adult auxiliary police discussed in Chapter Seven. The town would use about thirty youths, aged 17–21, to watch public areas such as schools, beaches, and parks to help cut down the amount of vandalism. The boys, following a training period in which they would attend seminars on delinquency and crime prevention, would be paid $2.50 an hour to scout vandal-prone areas from 7 P.M. to midnight on weekends during the school year and the same hours nightly during vacation. Dressed in identifying blazers, they would have no power of arrest but would only act as a strong deterrent.

A similar plan is being put into effect in Bedford-Stuyvesant, Brooklyn. Twenty-five men have been selected by the Brooklyn Model Cities Program and trained under the auspices of the Police Department. The green-uniformed Community Service Officers (CSO's) patrol parks and playgrounds on foot and on motor scooters in order to deter youth crime. They also have an ambulance at their disposal should they be called upon to give medical aid. The salaries for the CSO's, most of whom are blacks and Puerto Ricans, is $5,200 a year paid by the Brooklyn Model Cities Program.

"I'm excited for a number of reasons," Captain Kempner of the 79th Precinct told the *New York Times*. "These young men grew up in this neighborhood and they know what's going on. From the experience of their own lives, they know the problems of living here. They may be able to reach some of the kids."

Winston Ewbanks, a 21-year-old black veteran, agreed that the CSO's would be beneficial. "I think I'd be better than some white policeman because he's leading the good life out there on Long Island and he comes here and tells the people what to do." Mr. Ewbanks went on to say, "I think I can get respect from the kids because I'm younger."

The success of these plans is probable, as similar ideas using teen-agers have worked well throughout the country. In Washington, D.C., the District Health Department was on the verge of closing Knox Hill Health Clinic because of attacks by vandals. Windows were constantly being broken, constituting an emotional and physical threat to the patients. Patrols organized by other youths in the area eliminated the problem. In *Crime in the Suburbs*, David Loth tells about the town of Terra Linda in Marin County, California. The swimming pool and community center were under steady attack by vandals. Terra Linda officials closed the pool, saying there was no reason to keep it open if the people could not use it properly. Youngsters volunteered to repair the damaged property and since then have guarded it.

The whole area of beneficial youth involvement has yet to be explored fully. Considering the many out-of-work teen-agers who need employment that is manly, and appreciating the fact that youngsters might better understand the underlying reasons for vandalism than adults, the possibility of using young people in the fight seems worth investigating.

9

The Laws
and the Courts

"One, two, three,
That's how elementary it's going to be."
—*Madara–White–Borisoff*

In the realm of justice two conflicting philosophies
dominate: punishment versus rehabilitation. When
dealing with children, the philosophies become po-
larized to the point of bitter absurdity. In the past
we have had pre-teen children facing life imprison-
ment or even hung for minor crimes. The thinking
was that if the punishment was terrible enough,
youngsters would be discouraged from lawbreaking.

The advocates of this theory today see no problem.
If only people would get tough, there would be no
juvenile delinquency. It is as simple as that. A 1969
example in Florida was the 13- and 14-year-old boys
on their way to be placed in an adult prison with

hardened criminals until shocked public opinion forced the governor of the Sunshine State to prevent this. The boys' crime: incorrigibility.

On the other hand we have conditions as described in *Delinquency Can Be Stopped*. The authors, Judge Lester H. Loble and Max Wylie, felt a dangerous concept was widespread. One that held, "No youth should be punished for any crime, no matter how vicious; no youth is responsible for what he does—society alone is responsible."

The answer to the question of what is true justice would seem to lie between the two. People must take responsibility for their actions, be guided by laws, or else anarchy, young *and* old, will prevail. Yet the deeds of immature minds warrant a more thoughtful approach than the "eye for an eye" edict. After all, the world has become more civilized since the time boys were sent to debtors prison and died there as men.

In June 1872, the *New York Times* editorialized:

> We want reformatories deserving the name; not more taskhouses, where boys are put under lock and key, in the charge of ignorant and brutal jailers, but places where they are dealt with by a hand at once of the kindest and firmest, where they can be taught the impolicy of violence and wrong and be after a time put in the way of earning an honest livelihood.

111

A count two years later showed thirty-four reformatories in the United States with a total of 8,924 inmates (1,481 girls, 7,443 boys).

The feeling that children's crimes should be viewed differently from those of adults was evident in an 1874 plan to induce delinquent boys to sign up as midshipmen on one of the many ships frequenting New York Harbor. One wonders about the success of this idea. Echoes of such a philosophy are found in the Civilian Conservation Corps camps set up by President Franklin D. Roosevelt and the Job Corps Centers which tried to meet the needs of high school dropouts. Both modern ideas were designed to provide work or training in order to discourage aimless youth from drifting into crime. The premise is sound and reflects Paul Goodman's philosophy mentioned in Chapter Five that teen-age boys need manly jobs to feel worthwhile.

With the passage of the 1899 Juvenile Court Law in Chicago, the "understanding" philosophy took firm hold. Under this law, the Juvenile Court system was set up, designed to protect minors from the severity of adult laws and indirectly from judges who placed children and adult criminals in the same category. Delinquents at that time, according to the *U.S. News & World Report*, were seen as misguided children eager to respond to the fatherly hand of a judge. As will happen when justice is open to wide interpretation, however, some disparate judgments are made.

In March 1921, a White Plains, New York, judge instructed a 12-year-old boy who had stolen $13 worth of candy and cigarettes, "Don't eat any chocolate candy for a year; go to school every day, and attend mass every Sunday with the probation officer." What is interesting is that a probation officer in 1921 had time to attend church with his charges. Today, some probation officers have as many as four hundred cases. The only contact such a man has with his charge is sometimes an hour a month or merely a post card.

At the opposite end of the scale was Mayor A. R. Bergstrom of Coatesville, Pennsylvania. In June 1936, seventeen boys were apprehended for vandalism. Mayor Bergstrom told the parents that he would not turn the boys over to the juvenile authorities if the parents would "lick 'em right here in the police station."

"Fine idea," one father said.

The mayor told the newspapers, "Every boy got several lashes. The funny thing about it was that mothers were more severe in the whipping than the fathers."

The above examples are the extremes. More balanced is the June 1964 decision of the Lehigh County Juvenile Court of Pennsylvania. Five Allentown boys were arrested for wrecking a park. According to the *Eagle* of Reading, the court sentenced the boys to work off the cost of the damage: $735.60. The culprits were also put on a two-year probation, had to observe a strict 9:30 P.M. curfew, had their driver's licenses confiscated, and were ordered to avoid bad company in general and the company of each other specifically.

An *Eagle* editorial reasoned, "Such a 'wreckers-must-work-it-off' idea just might curb vandalism elsewhere. It's worth a try, it seems to us."

The Louisville and Nashville Railroad would agree. The railroad had a bill of $15,000 for broken signal lights. The company reported they never had a repeater when the vandal was caught and had to make reimbursement.

Some vandalism is committed by children who have no idea of the replacement cost. As the editor of the Hartford, Connecticut, *Times* stated, "To a child who has never had to earn his pleasure, a pane of glass is of inconsiderable value. If he learns that it must be paid for in terms of hard work and deprivation of ice cream and movies he has some appreciation of its real cost."

The matter of restitution for acts of vandals by minors has been the source of a long-standing debate. Some people feel that if parents were forced to pay part or all the cost of the damage done by their children, they would supervise their sons and daughters more closely. As a result there would be less vandalism. Arguments date from October 9, 1880, when the *New York Times* said, "Fines are a punishment to the parents and not to the child and, besides, the result would be that the well-to-do would pay and the poor ones would let their children go to jail in default. Indubitably, however, the parent who paid a fine would make his son smart for it when he got home,"—to a letter to the editor of the *Times*, October 8, 1964: "If fathers were sent to jail and had to pay the costs of damage, there would be a very swift drop in such activities."

The theory brings to mind what a teacher in a school for military dependents told a friend. "Never mind all that stuff you hear about service brats. We have no serious discipline problems. First, we speak to the parents. If that doesn't help, we notify the principal who alerts the commanding officer. The C.O. speaks to the father. You'd be surprised how fast the problem vanishes."

So the idea of putting pressure on parents to alleviate certain youth problems might have merit. Residents of forty-two states believe this as they have liability laws requiring parents of vandals to pay up to a set sum. Usually the amount is $250 to $500, though Texas has a ruling that can force parents to pay as high as $5,000.

New York City, urged by groups such as the High School Teachers Association, has tried since 1959 to pass a bill to make parents pay $25. The rule has never become a law.

New York State has been no more successful.

In 1955, both the Assembly and the Senate approved a bill that would make parents financially responsible up to $250 for children 16 years old or younger. Governor Harriman vetoed it for two reasons. The burden would fall particularly hard on low-income families and the liability for parents who could pay more would be limited by the set sum.

The New York State Bar Association supported a 1960 bill which proposed the same sum as in 1955. The Bar felt the law "may act as a deterrent and perhaps bring about a greater parental supervision." The law was opposed by social welfare groups because they felt an unfair economic strain would be placed on families that could ill afford it, increasing the already weakened family bonds. For the third time in five years the Assembly approved the bill only to have the Senate kill it.

More recently, State Senator Edward J. Speno has tried to have a liability law passed in New York State. On November 25, 1968, and December 18, 1968, Senator Speno held Public Hearings in Rochester and Buffalo respectively, to take testimony on the prospective bill which set a monetary limit of five hundred dollars. The testimony at those hearings sums up the arguments on the entire question.

NEW YORK CITY COMPTROLLER MARIO PROCACCINO. "I do believe that the imposition of civil liability might be appropriate in such cases where it is shown that the parent—either expressly or implied—condones such vandalous acts of the child." Comptroller Procaccino went on to explain after questions were raised that "implied" meant that the parents know the child is prone to vandalism but do nothing about it. "Expressly" is where the parents see the act and do not stop it. "If a child has a wrong sense of values, it is largely the fault of the parent in condoning the child's wrongful conduct," added Procaccino.

But not everyone agreed.

MR. NICHOLAS KISBURG—TEAMSTERS UNION. ". . . I think it is unconstitutional because . . . poor people won't pay, only rich people . . . and it has always been my belief that class justice is unconstitutional in New York State."

STANLEY J. RUBIN—LEGISLATURE CHAIRMAN OF THE NEW YORK STATE ASSOCIATION OF TRIAL LAWYERS. "Parents pay enough, I think, with heartache and grief and worry and concern."

MR. JUSTICE FRIEMUND, NEW YORK DIRECTOR OF THE
NATIONAL COUNCIL ON CRIME AND DELINQUENCY. Mr.
Friemund took no definite stand but he did point
out that "frequently it [a liability law] results in
probation officers and other people involved with
the Family Court and others taking on additional
duties of bill collecting."

But most of the testimony at both hearings was in
favor of the passage of such a bill.

LAWRENCE M. QUINLAN, SHERIFF OF DUTCHESS
COUNTY, NEW YORK. "A pretty sad situation when
decent living people have their property destroyed
and in court the judge has no power to place the
responsibility of paying for the damage on anyone. . . ."

DR. P. MARION, KINGS COUNTY COMMITTEE TO SUP-
PORT YOUR LOCAL POLICE. Dr. Marion pointed out that
it was difficult to get insurance because we now have
vandalism without compensation. He posed the possibility that insurance rates might go down if companies knew someone would be financially responsible for the destruction.

EUGENE KELLY, SPOKESMAN FOR COMMISSIONER
JOHN L. BARRY, SUFFOLK COUNTY POLICE DEPARTMENT.
Kelly described a meeting of representatives of fifty

school boards from Suffolk County where the vandalism problem had been explored in depth. Every person at the meeting approved of the bill Senator Speno was sponsoring. One Suffolk school district had recently spent $56,000 for radar-sensing devices to alert police to vandals and thieves. "Only if you hit the individual parent in the pocketbook does he or she make any effort to control their offspring, or does he or she take any steps to find out exactly where their children are when they go out at night."

After the hearings, Senators Speno, Hughes, Laverne, and Lombardi submitted a bill that would make it possible for the court to require a vandal to (1) "obtain such employment as the court shall direct in a capacity that will benefit the health, safety and welfare of the general public; and/or (2) make restitution in an amount not to exceed five hundred dollars, for any damage done to the property of another person." And this bill, also, would make parents responsible for damage not "in excess of the sum of five hundred dollars" if a similar penalty had not been imposed on the vandal.

The bill was vetoed.

A month later Senators Marino, Caemmerer, Dunne, Lent, and Speno submitted a revised bill. The sum was lowered to $250 "for parents, guardians, or other persons having legal custody of a minor child between the ages of ten and eighteen years."

The possibility of such bills becoming law is greater now than in the past because as the *U.S. News & World Report* noted in March 1969, "A stern attitude toward youthful offenders has been growing." Several telling incidents would substantiate this theory.

In 1961 a Montana judge, Lester H. Loble, sponsored a state law that would radically change the procedure of handling juvenile criminals. Across the United States the present way of dealing with youngsters under 16 is to charge them with Juvenile Delinquency rather than a specific crime. From 16 to 19, young people charged with a crime may ask for Youthful Offender Treatment so that their trial is not on public record and no publicity is released to any of the news media. The matter of public record is important should the boys in later life ever wish to apply for a civil service job or to seek entrance to the Bar. They would be denied the position due to a criminal record.

In terms of vandalism those 16 and up are charged with three degrees of Criminal Mischief.

Types	Crime	Penalty
3rd Degree	Damage under $250	Not over 1 year
2nd Degree	Exceeding $250	Not over 4 years
1st Degree	$1,500—and using explosives	Not over 7 years

Judge Lester H. Loble labored under these pro-
visions and observed that many young men released
from his court were back in less than a month on
the same charge. Most juvenile cases were handled
with care, thought, and with the goal of rehabilitating
the boy, but Judge Loble could not see people like
the boys who found a drunken bum unconscious on
a Helena, Montana, street, escaping punishment.
They had sprayed the man with inflammable liquid
and set him afire. The boys sought Youthful Offender
Treatment to protect themselves. The judge was
more concerned about who would "protect" the people of his state from such individuals. So he drew up
a state bill, proposing open hearings for felons. A
felony is a crime against a person, as opposed to a
misdemeanor which is a crime against property. A
vandal is not a felon, but the general attitude toward
youthful criminals will affect the handling of a person convicted of Criminal Mischief.

Even in the conservative West, it is not easy to
change the people's philosophy toward the law.
Judge Loble saw his bill sent to committee in the
state legislature and stay there. Only one thing could
save his bill. Go right to the people. Touring all of
Montana, he spoke to lodges, farm groups, ranchers,
bankers, miners, PTA's, prisons, and churches. He
even made appearances in stores. When his bill was
re-introduced, it passed the House 89 to 6. In the

Senate the vote was 56 for—with only one vote against. The Loble Law went into effect in 1961.

Subsequently, the trials of juveniles charged with a felony in Montana were open, which meant that the public could attend the hearing, though no cameras are allowed. The name, address, exact description of the crime, full background of the offender, his parents' names, his father's occupation, the school record of the offender, are all permitted to be used by the news media.

Cries of "Hanging Judge" rose from several quarters, but a closer inspection of the judge's handling of youthful criminals shows that his justice is tempered with understanding. If he thinks the offense is not a serious one, and if he finds the boy has a good record, he will try the case informally, in secret, at the misdemeanor level without publicity. While this law appears to be working well under Judge Loble's supervision, the other side of the issue should be voiced. What will happen if a more vindictive judge uses his power poorly? Some youthful lawbreakers might have their lives ruined by an act they committed when they were too young to appreciate the future consequences.

The results of the Loble Law?

Several important things have happened in Judge Loble's estimation:

1. The law has helped restore the people's confidence in the courts.

2. The law is fair to decent youngsters. Good teenagers are not suffering from the reputation of the bad.

3. More parents are paying proper attention to their children.

All the positive effects are not merely the opinion of the law's creator. A recent look at the figures of arrest of persons under 18 for serious crimes show that across the country the figure jumped 47% above the 1960 figures. But in Montana the average for the same period dropped 49%, even though the population growth went up 17%.

Though the inspiration may not have come from Montana, the state of New Jersey lifted the ban on press reports about Juvenile Court proceedings in 1965. At the discretion of the judges, the names, photographs, and other identifying data of offenders are available for release. Radio and TV may use this information, too, but no broadcasting is permitted from the courtroom.

Despite what some people feel, penalties do not eradicate crime. If dissolution was that easy, crime would have vanished a long time ago. A trend toward sterner treatment of juvenile offenders may well be in motion, however. People are alarmed at the rate of youth crime, and law and order have become key words for any hopeful politician. If the pendulum is swinging, the tremendous vandalism problem may be supplying part of the propelling force.

10

Some Answers

"Will time make men more wise?"
—*Samwell-Smith–Relf–McCarthy*

Help and *assistance.* A thesaurus lists fifteen other words all having a similar meaning to help and assistance. Whichever synonym seems preferable, the plain fact is that help is now needed to make this country aware of the vandalism problem—so acutely aware that everyone will work together to fight the situation. In the past young Americans have taken the lead in combatting contemporary issues such as civil rights, the quest for peace, and environmental contamination. Now their assistance is needed to stop the rising vandalism rate. After all—isn't vandalism another dangerous form of environmental decay? Smog and polluted water attack the cells and organs of the body. Vandalism corrodes a man's social pride.

The discussion of Erosive Vandalism in Chapter Three indicated how the effect of a depersonalized environment works detrimentally on the inhabitants. How can anyone—young or old—feel a part of an area when they see 100-year-old oaks sawed down in road-widening programs, or the stores they frequent one week crushed by the wrecker's ball the next week? Why wouldn't youngsters write on walls or pull apart playground apparatus, figuring these may be the next to vanish in this uncaring world? Why should grownups worry about litter or what their children ruin? Let that unseen, governing agency take care of the mess. As the physical appearance deteriorates, so does the inhabitants' desire to treat the property respectfully. The two conditions are linked in a downward spiral which is almost impossible to stop once started.

But not *impossible.*

Paul Goodman wrote in *Growing Up Absurd:* "Modern times have been characterized by fundamental changes occurring with unusual rapidity. These have shattered tradition but often have not succeeded in creating a new whole community. We have no recourse to going back, there is nothing to go back to."

So we must go forward. New solutions need to be found to fight vandalism. The problem is twofold.

Some Answers

Youngsters have to appreciate the financial and moral price extracted by vandalism, as most vandals are in their teens or younger. Adults have to become equally involved so that many of the previously discussed conditions that motivate the not-so-senseless crime can be changed. How can a young person wage such a two-prong attack on the apathetic population? Here are some beginning suggestions which might be helpful or even inspire more exciting methods.

FOR ELEMENTARY STUDENTS: Primary grade children are still most influenced by their parents and teachers. Classroom lessons about the dangers of vandalism greatly affect first, second, and third graders. When their parents tell them how terrible vandalism is, these children believe it. But as the youngsters grow older, they are more easily swayed by older brothers or sisters in junior and senior high school than by adults. That is when these 9-, 10-, and 11-year-olds adopt pseudo-teen-age mannerisms and dress. Unfortunately, they mostly hear stories about how much fun it is to get into trouble or engage in activities frowned upon by grownups. So the children begin to think that misbehavior is synonymous with growing up.

Wouldn't it be great if these youngsters had some high school students visit their classroom and "level" with them about how "dumb" it was to go around breaking school windows and doing other destructive acts? Some honest, down-to-earth talk from teen-agers reflecting upon their own past vandalistic acts would be more effective than the same words from an adult.

The elementary pupils might be so impressed they would ask their teacher if they could plan an assembly program for the other classes and the parents, a show about vandalism in their home town. They could write and perform their own plays. Or the teacher might want to organize a school-wide social studies or citizenship education fair similar to the very popular science fairs. At a Social Studies Fair students would prepare murals and dioramas and table-top models depicting community problems such as vandalism.

A nucleus of sincere teen-agers would be welcomed by the elementary schools and could set into motion many activities. The effect would reach not only the younger children but the community as a whole.

FOR JUNIOR AND SENIOR HIGH SCHOOL STUDENTS: There are several activities which would be fun as well as productive for teen-agers in junior and senior high school who wish to make fellow students and adults aware of vandalism.

Now that film-making has become such a widespread hobby, photographic exhibitions would enable amateur photographers to put their talent to a good use. Both still photographs and motion pictures of community decay would be enlightening. A person can walk or drive past a mutilated stop sign day after day without truly noticing it. But a 9×12 enlargement, skillfully mounted, showing the bullet holes and the twisted, rusting metal, would sharply illustrate the issue.

Photography could be incorporated into another means of alerting people to the spread of vandalism. Many high school drama clubs or senior classes perform at least one stage production a year. Why not do a rock musical? Many contemporary songs are message songs, dealing with man's misuse of the earth. These might comprise the musical score, or else original songs could be composed by the rock groups which exist in every high school today. If the school is near a college, an English or drama major might be eager to write the "book" for the musical, or, again, some high school students could handle the writing chore. Scenery could be projected slides and motion pictures dealing with vandalism on all levels. Exciting stage lighting, utilizing strobe lights or ultraviolet spotlights, would complete the multimedia show.

FOR THOSE EIGHTEEN OR OLDER: The trend in both England and Scotland, as well as the United States, is toward lowering the voting age. Young people can now have a more active voice in determining those laws which affect them. This power might be used to insist that there be more public involvement in community planning. Do the people want those 100-year-old trees removed or would they prefer some pleasant roads through their town? Which does the village need more? A new block of stores which admittedly brings in more tax money but offers no new services to an area which already has two barber shops and three food markets? Or a field that can be alternately used for organized sports or running mini-bikes?

At one time only property owners had a voice in deciding these matters. More and more, as shown in school elections which are now open to *all* eligible voters, everyone is clamoring for a right to speak. And the young people will have a decisive hand— if they want to use it.

Another way that young people can support the campaign against vandalism is protest. Groups now picket chemical companies because these factories produce war supplies. What about indicating our displeasure with those industrial concerns that are polluting the atmosphere, the waters, and the earth itself with industrial wastes? Why not a concerted drive to urge other businesses to take an active part in the fight against vandalism? Companies might employ the tax-free dollars that are available for organizations producing films and other educative materials. The need exists for free, elementary-school-child oriented materials as well as some geared for teen-agers and adult consumption. What about the possibility of TV specials like the Bell Telephone series which first presented hour-long programs such as "Our Mr. Sun" and "Hemo the Magnificent" (about blood) on television and then made them available without charge to schools?

Other methods can be devised by which companies might fight vandalism. The Adolph Coors Company of Golden, Colorado, pays 1¢ for every empty Coors beer can or bottle that is returned, and they do this at a *loss* of ½¢ each. In only one year, the Coors Company collected 12 million aluminum cans and 104 million bottles. Deservedly, the company received a GOMA (Good Outdoor Manners Association) Award.

This is another way groups can help in the fight against vandals. Organizations besides GOMA of Seattle might present awards to those individuals or companies deserving notice. In addition they could nominate the inconsiderate, destructive people for a negative citation. One group of riflemen received such an undesirable nomination from GOMA. The unknown hunters slaughtered 100 sea lions on Santa

Barbara Island, California, and then blew up the unattended ranger station. Mass media could aid the struggle by giving exposure to the awards.

Perhaps the most needed weapon in the fight against vandalism is a national organization which would act as a clearing house for information about the crime. The funds for the council could come from the Federal government or possibly an organization such as the Ford Foundation.

Right now if Machias, Maine, or Colon, Michigan, or Bowie, Maryland, find their communities plagued with vandalism, they have to begin from point zero in their attempt to combat the problem. The town may decide to hold a vandal panel only to learn too late that panels are ineffective. So valuable time and energy is wasted at the beginning of the anti-vandalism drive, a time when the most people are the most aroused. This happens because villages have been fighting separately. No one learns or profits from cooperation. The result is a losing battle against vandalism.

But if a nationwide council collated reports from across the United States and recorded unsuccessful as well as positive methods utilized in different communities, the time factor would be changed and very possibly so would the odds of winning the fight. This council would be a clearing house for the latest research on vandalism. If the financial backing was great enough, such an organization might be able to send experienced field experts to aid citizen groups in high-incidence areas.

Despite all these aforementioned techniques for acquainting people with the extent of vandalism, no significant change will occur until the individual corporation—and the person—acts differently. When 7-year-old Kevin realizes it is wrong to mar the park statue and puts away his crayons unused—when a college student decides not to rip out a restaurant booth for the Zap bonfire—when one boy refuses to join the gang attacking the Ryans' house—that's the time the spread of vandalism will be halted. Until that happens, the effort to stop the not-so-senseless crime deserves all our energy—

> For such maliciousness is not only destructive to property. It is destructive to personal discipline and the sense of responsibility. Carried to extremes, it could destroy orderly society itself.
> —*Tribune*
> Salt Lake City, Utah

Sources and Suggested Readings

Vandalism produces many problems. One of them not often mentioned is the problem of research. Thousands of newspaper articles are available but they become repetitive. Magazine articles seeking to explore the crime base their conclusions on the same few sources and often end up quoting each other. Much of the material in *Vandalism: The Not-So-Senseless Crime* has come from newspapers and first-hand interviews. This makes it difficult for the person seeking to do more in-depth readings in any particular area. Below is a *very* selective list of sources as well as additional leads that interested people might want to follow. Hopefully, there will soon be more books on the topic.

Chapter 1. *vandals and Vandals*

Bridgewater, William, and Kurtz, Seymour, *Columbia Encyclopedia*. New York, Columbia University Press, 1963. pg. 2227.

Bury, J. B., *The Invasion of Europe by the Barbarians*. New York, Russell & Russell, 1963. pp. 103–5, 160–61.

"The Ravaged Environment," *Newsweek*, Vol. LXXV No. 4 (January 26, 1970), pp. 30–47.

"Surging Vandalism," *U.S. News & World Report*, Vol. LXVII No. 8 (August 25, 1969), pp. 32–34.

Chapter 2. *Back Then and Over There*

Cain, Dr. Arthur H., *Young People and Crime*. New York, The John Day Company, 1968.

Graham, Hugh Davis, and Gurr, Ted Robert, *Violence in America*. New York, Bantam Books, 1969. pp. 45–76.

Lancaster, Bruce, *From Lexington to Liberty*. New York, Doubleday & Company, Inc., 1955. pp. 52–54.

Niles, Hezekiah, *Chronicles of the American Revolution*. New York, Grosset & Dunlap, 1965. pp. 67–68.

Chapter 3. *Erosive Vandalism*

Kazmier, Arnold, "Looking for America on the Living Desert," *The Village Voice*, September 11, 1969.

Loth, David, *Crime in the Suburbs*. New York, William Morrow, 1967. pp. 98–116.

Sources and Suggested Readings

Chapter 4. *Fun Vandalism*

Bennett, Joseph W., *Vandals Wild*. Portland, Bennett Publishing Company, 1969.

Tunley, Roul, *Kids, Crime and Chaos*. New York, Harper and Brothers, 1962.

Chapter 5. *Angry Vandalism*

Friedenberg, Edgar Z., *Coming of Age in America*. New York, Random House, 1963.

U.S. Riot Commission Report: Report of the National Advisory Commission on Civil Disorders. New York, Bantam Books, 1968.

Saul, Leon J., *The Hostile Mind*. New York, Random House, 1956.

Stein, Edward V., *The Stranger Inside You*. Philadelphia, The Westminster Press, 1965. pp. 154–208.

Storr, Anthony, *Human Aggression*. New York, Atheneum, 1968.

Chapter 6. *Community Reaction*

Fromm, Eric, *The Sane Society*. New York, Holt, Rinehart & Winston, 1955.

Goldman, Nathan, *A Socio-Psychological Study of School Vandalism*. Syracuse, Syracuse University Press, 1959.

Greenstein, Raymond, "Can We Lessen Vandalism?", *The Instructor*, Vol. LXXIX No. 5 (January 1970), pp. 90–91.

Kvaraceus, William C., *Juvenile Delinquency*. Washington, National Education Association, 1958.

Chapter 7. *Vigilantism and Auxiliary Police*

Graham, Hugh Davis, and Gurr, Ted Robert, *Violence in America*. New York, Bantam Books, 1969.

Nassau County Police Department Rules—Regulations and Procedures for Civil Defense Auxiliary Police. Mineola, Nassau County Police Department, 1968.

Chapter 8. *Peer Reaction*

"Wreckreation," *Senior Scholastic*, 90 (May 12, 1967), pp. 21–23.

Chapter 9. *The Laws and the Courts*

"Crisis in Juvenile Courts," *U.S. News & World Report*, Vol. LXVI No. 12 (March 24, 1969), p. 62.

Loble, Judge Lester H., and Wylie, Max, *Delinquency Can Be Stopped*. New York, McGraw-Hill Book Company, 1967.

"Your Son Is Arrested for Vandalism," *McCalls*, 96 (April 1969), p. 74.

Chapter 10. *Some Answers*

Goodman, Paul, *Growing Up Absurd*. New York, Random House, 1960.

"The Vandal: Society's Outsider," *Time*, Vol. 93 No. 3 (January 19, 1970), pp. 45–46.

OTHER SOURCES

A. *General Readings:*

Brown, Claude, *Manchild in the Promised Land.* New York, The Macmillan Company, 1965.

Cleaver, Eldridge, *Soul on Ice.* New York, McGraw-Hill Book Company, 1968.

Friedenberg, Edgar Z., *The Vanishing Adolescent.* Boston, Beacon Press, 1959.

Goodman, Paul, *Compulsory MIS-education.* New York, Horizon Press, 1964.

Goodman, Paul, *Like a Conquered Province.* New York, Random House, 1966.

Gordon, Richard E. and Katherine K., and Gunther, Max, *The Split Level Trap.* New York, Bernard Geis, 1961.

Keats, John, *The Crack in the Picture Window.* Boston, Houghton Mifflin Company, 1956.

Martin, John M., *Juvenile Vandalism.* Springfield, Ill., Charles C Thomas, 1961.

Wertheim, Fredric, *Sign for Cain.* New York, Macmillan Company, 1966.

B. *Films:*

"Mike Makes His Mark," 29 minutes, color, National Education Association, 1201 Sixteenth Street, N.W., Washington, D.C.

Vandalism

"Homer and Bill Fight the Vandals," 5-minute slide show, National Association of Home Builders, 1625 L Street, N.W., Washington, D.C. 20036.

C. Organizations:

National Council on Crime and Delinquency
44 East 23rd Street
New York, N.Y. 10018

The NCCD has a library open for public use of materials connected with crime and juvenile delinquency. Books may be taken out with proof of identification.

ACKNOWLEDGMENTS

Grateful acknowledgment is made to the following publishers and authors for permission to use copyrighted material from the titles listed:

THE CHRONICLES OF THE AMERICAN REVOLUTION, edited by Hezekiah Niles. Copyright © 1965 Grosset & Dunlap, Inc. Publishers.

GROWING UP ABSURD, by Paul Goodman. Copyright © 1960 by Random House, Inc. Used by permission.

HUMAN AGGRESSION by Anthony Storr. Copyright © 1968 by Anthony Storr. Reprinted by permission of Atheneum Publishers.

OUR TOWN by Thornton Wilder. Copyright © 1938, 1957 by Thornton Wilder, Harper & Row. Reprinted by permission.

THE STRANGER INSIDE YOU, by Edward V. Stein. Copyright © MCMLXV, W. L. Jenkins, The Westminster Press. Used by permission.

In addition the author wishes to acknowledge permission to quote the lyrics of the following songs:

FOR WHAT IT'S WORTH by Stephen Stills. © 1967 by Cotillion Music, Inc., Ten East Music and Springalo Toones. Used by permission.

GOOD MORNING, GOOD MORNING by John Lennon and Paul McCartney. Copyright © 1967 by Northern Songs Limited. Used by permission. All rights reserved.

THE HOUSE OF THE RISING SUN by Alan Price. Copyright © 1964 by Keith Prowse Music Publishing Co. Ltd., 21 Denmark Street, London, W.C. 2, England, for the Entire World. All rights for the U.S.A. and Canada controlled by Al Gallico Music Corporation, 101 West 55th Street, New York, N.Y. 10019. International Copyright secured. All rights reserved.

MIND TIME by Heend and Ross. Copyright © 1965 by Crescendo Songs, Inc. Used by permission.

SHAPES OF THINGS by Samwell-Smith, Relf, McCarthy. Copyright © 1966 by B. Feldman & Co. Ltd., London, England. All rights for the U.S.A. and Canada controlled by Unart Music Corporation, New York, N.Y. Used by permission.

YOU'VE GOT YOUR TROUBLES by Roger & Roger. Copyright © 1965 by Mills Music Ltd. Used by permission.

ONE, TWO, THREE by John Madara, David White, Leonard Borisoff. Copyright © 1965 by Champion Music Corporation and Double Diamond Music Corporation, New York, N.Y. Used by permission. All rights reserved.

THOSE WERE THE DAYS, words and music by Gene Raskin. TRO—Copyright © 1968 by Essex Music, Inc., New York, N.Y. Used by permission.

Index

Adult vandals, 45–46
Aggression: vandalism as outlet for, 53–57
Allentown, Pa., 113–14
Angry vandalism, 48–65, 103–5
Anti-Semitism, 19–20, 59
Anti-war protests, 18–19, 50, 58
Assaults, 50, 89
Automobiles, 16, 17, 21, 30–31, 40, 45, 51, 52, 83, 87–88, 89; abandoned, 36; tires, 17, 30, 59, 103

Bars and taverns, 5, 39
Beaches, 57, 92
Bergstrom, A. R., 113
Bio-Research Institute, 4
Boise (Idaho) *Evening Statesmen*, 42
Bombing, 51
Boston, Mass., 13
Boston Tea Party, 11–13, 62
Bottles: disposal of, 133; smashing, 21, 26, 101
Brookhaven, N. Y., 80
Brooklyn, N. Y., 87, 108–9
Brown, Richard Maxwell, *The History of Violence in America*, 11, 85, 87
Buffalo, N. Y., 45–46

Cain, Arthur H., *Young People and Crime*, quoted, 10, 20
Cairo, Ill., 89
Cambridge, Mass., 4
Central Islip, N. Y., 87
Chemicals, 4

Churches and synagogues, 5, 19–20, 59–61, 96
Civil rights movement, 61–64
Cleveland, O., 89
Cleveland *Plain Dealer*, 38
Coatesville, Pa., 113
College-age vandals, 21, 38–40, 55, 58
Collins, George R., 91–98
Cologne, Germany, 19–20
Communities, action to prevent vandalism, 71–84
Connecticut, 32, 57, 81, 83
Connell, Edward A., quoted, 28
Conventions, 45–46
Courts, 110–24
Curfews, 17–18, 82–84, 114

Dogs, guard, 75–76
Dooley, Kenneth J., 83
Drunkenness, 21, 97, 121

Embassies, 19
Erosive vandalism, 25–36, 103, 128
Ewbanks, Winston, 108–9

Fires, 39–40, 42, 61, 64, 69–72, 89
Florida, 21, 39, 83, 110–11
Fort Lauderdale, Fla., 21, 39
Fraser, Scott, 30–31
Friedenberg, Edgar Z., quoted, 56
Friemund, Justice, quoted, 118
Fromm, Eric, *The Sane Society*, 77

Index

Fuchs, Norman, 38, 40
Fun vandalism, 37–47, 103
Furniture, destruction of, 7, 39, 58, 59, 89

Garbage, 35, 36, 51
Ghettos, riots and vandalism in, 62–65
Glueck, Sheldon S. and Eleanor T., 37–38
Goldman, Nathan, 74
Good Outdoor Manners Association, 133
Goodman, Paul: *Growing Up Absurd*, 40, 55, 58, 102, 112, 128; *Like a Conquered Province*, quoted, 5–6
Graffiti, 33–34
Greenstein, Raymond, 73

Halloween vandalism, 43–45, 98
Hartford *Times*, 114
Hastings-on-Hudson, N. Y., 17–18
Hollywood, Calif., 83
Holy Loch, Scotland, 18
Homburger, Dr. Freddy, 4
Houses and private property, 7, 29, 32, 39, 50, 63–64, 81, 89, 92
Huntington, N. Y., 107–8

Insight, 71
Instructor, 73

Jakarta, Indonesia, 19
Jews, 60, 85, 86–87; *see also* Anti-Semitism, Churches and synagogues
Juvenile delinquents, 20–21, 32, 37–38, 56; laws and courts, 110–24

Kazmier, Arnold, 29

Kelly, Eugene, 118–19
Kisburg, Nicholas, quoted, 117
Kvaraceus, William C., quoted, 78

Lake Grove, N. Y., 89
Lichter, Solomon, quoted, 40–41
Linden, N. J., 7
Litter, 27, 33, 34–35, 57
Loble, Lester H., 120–23
Loble, Lester H. and Max Wylie, *Delinquency Can Be Stopped*, quoted, 111
Long Island, N. Y., vandalism in, 5–7, 16, 17–18, 41, 48–50, 71, 72, 79–80, 87, 89, 90, 101, 107–8
Looney, Francis·B., 32, 44
Looting of stores, 39, 61, 81
Los Angeles *Times*, 71, 107
Loth, David, *Crime in the Suburbs*, 32, 109

Marion, P., 118
Massapequa, N. Y., 71, 79–80
Middletown, Conn., 81, 83
Minorities, 59–60, 85, 86–87
Montana, juvenile delinquent law, 120–23
Monuments and memorials, 18, 19, 33, 46
Murphy, Richard, 45

Narcotics addicts, 46, 64–65, 72
Nassau County, N. Y.: Neighborhood Security Program, 31–32; Police Department, 31, 41, 44, 63, 90–98; vandalism in, 48–50, 71, 79–80, 87, 101, 107–8
National Advisory Commission on Civil Disorders, quoted, 62

Index

Negro vandals, 61–64, 81, 83, 86–87
Negro-white encounters, 81, 82, 86–87, 89
New Canaan, Conn., 32
New Haven, Conn., 57
New York City, 8, 108; vandalism in, 14, 27, 29–30, 46, 116
New York *Daily News*, 59, 65
New York State, 5–7, 16, 17–18, 41, 45–46, 48–50, 71, 73, 79–80, 87, 89, 90, 99, 101, 107–8, 113, 118–19; law on liability of parents, 115–17
New York Times, 14, 15–16, 28, 38, 52, 59, 63, 86, 112, 115

Oakland, Calif., 34
Old Ironsides (ship), 13
Oregon, 100
Oslo, Norway, 22

Pacific Palisades, Calif., 51
Paint, defacement with, 7, 16, 18–20, 45, 59
Parents: attitudes on vandalism, 33–34, 43–44, 70, 73, 76, 101, 102, 105, 106, 113, 129; and children, 33–34, 44, 46–47, 52, 55, 65, 102, 104–5; restitution for vandalism of children, 114–19
Parks, 7, 27, 33, 42, 46–47, 59, 92–93, 113
Pawtucket, R. I., 28
Plainedge, N. Y., 87
Plainview, N. Y., 99
Police, 16, 17, 20, 31, 41, 44, 49–50, 57, 61, 63, 89, 119; auxiliary, 89–98, 107–8
Police Athletic League, 56
Political vandalism, 11–13, 18–19

Pollution and depersonalization of environment, 7, 8, 29, 30, 32
Pretoria, South Africa, 19
Procaccino, Mario, quoted, 117
Protests, 18–19, 50, 58, 83
Proteus (submarine), 18
Punishment for vandalism, 110–24

Quinlan, Lawrence M., quoted, 118

Railroads, 7, 22, 41–42, 114
Reading (Pa.) *Eagle*, 114
Recreation: centers, 65, 80–82; importance to teen-agers, 55–56, 65
Robbery, 21, 92, 97, 103
Rock-throwing, 7, 42
Rubin, Stanley J., quoted, 117
Ryan, Mr. and Mrs. John H., 48–50

Salt Lake City (Utah) *Tribune*, 135
Schools, 93; and prevention of vandalism, 73–76, 77, 107, 129–31; vandalism in, 5, 6–7, 16, 51, 58, 69–70, 73, 74, 81, 99–100, 101
Senior Scholastic, 78, 106
Shuval, Judith T., 20–21
Signs, 17, 103; *see also* Street and traffic signs
Speno, Edward J., 116, 119
Spring Valley, N. Y., 16
Squires, Donald, 7
Statues, 25–26, 135
Stein, Edward V., *The Stranger Inside You*, 54
Stonehenge, England, 18
Storr, Anthony, *Human Aggression*, 53–54

147

Index

Street and traffic signs, 5, 7, 16, 27, 100–1, 131; *see also* Signs
Suffolk County, N. Y., 41, 80, 87, 90, 118–19
Synagogues, *see* Churches and synagogues
Syosset, N. Y., 47
Syracuse, N. Y., 73

Teen-agers: activities in combating vandalism, 106–9, 127–31; and aggression, 53–57; attitudes on vandalism, 99–105; and growth to maturity, 51–58; influence of older on younger children, 47, 100, 129; pent-up anger and frustrations of, 52, 53, 57–58, 63, 73
Teen-age vandals, 10, 20, 28, 32, 37–38, 46–47, 48–50, 78–79, 87, 100–2, 113–14; definition, xi, 62; reason for vandalism, 42–43, 52–58; typical, 62
Telephones, 7, 22, 28
Terra Linda, Calif., 109
Thompson, Clara, 53–54
Time, 101
Tombstones and graves, 7, 16, 20
Tunley, Roul, *Kids, Crime and Chaos,* 37

Union, N. J., 16–17, 51
U. S. News and World Report, 5, 112, 120

Vandal, origin of word, 3–4
Vandalism: attacks on problem of, 9, 31–32, 65, 69–98, 105–9, 114–19, 127–35; attitudes toward, 5, 42–43; causes of and motivations for, 15, 21, 22, 25–65, 100, 102; contemporary problem of, 4–5, 15, 25, 99–109, 127–35; cost of, 5, 6, 8, 21, 41, 51, 60, 72, 75, 100, 101, 114, 119; definitions of, 9; history and development of, 11–21; types of, 25–65
Vandals (tribe), 3–4
Vandals: ages of, 78; attitudes of, 27, 31, 40–41, 52–58, 99–109; *see also* Teen-age vandals
Vermont, 36
Vigilantism, 85–89
Village Voice, 29
Violence: positive, 11, 61–62; types of, 11

Waldman, Albert A., 38
Walls, defacement of, 7, 16, 20, 21, 29, 39, 61, 64, 99, 103, 128
Washington, D. C., 58, 61, 109
Wertham, Fredric, *A Sign for Cain,* quoted, 8
Westbury, N. Y., 101
White Plains, N. Y., 113
Wilder, Thornton, *Our Town,* quoted, 15
Window breakage, 6–7, 17, 21, 27, 28, 50, 62, 64, 74, 81, 87, 101–2, 109, 114, 130
Works of art, 58
World vandalism, 20–22

Yellowstone National Park, 46
Yosemite Valley, 35
Youth commissions and boards, 76–80

Zap, N. D., 38–40, 135
Zimbardo, Philip, 30–31